LABYRINTH OF DREAMS

She has a dream. He has a plan.
But an unexpected secret child could destroy everything.

NADEE FERNANDO O'DRISCOLL

Labyrinth of Dreams

She has a dream. He has a plan.
But an unexpected secret child could
destroy everything.

Nadee Fernando-O'Driscoll

✤ LUCKY BOOK PUBLISHING

Published by Lucky Book Publishing: www.luckybookpublishing.com

To request permissions, contact the publisher at hello@luckybookpublishing.com.

Hardcover ISBN: 978-1-998287-28-4
Paperback ISBN: 978-1-998287-27-7
E-book ISBN: 978-1-998287-29-1

1st edition, September 2024.

"If people are doubting how far you can go, go so far that you can't hear them anymore."

~ **Michele Ruiz**

MY GIFT TO YOU

I am so glad you're here!

As my Gift to you, get FREE Access to the
Audiobook Labyrinth of Dreams
by scanning the QR Code below or visiting

https://nadeefernando-odriscoll.com/

ACKNOWLEDGMENTS

This book is dedicated to every person, especially young girls who stand their ground, hold on to their dreams and fight for their freedoms. I salute you for your strength and courage in choosing to be who you are: unique and powerful. Neither conformed to, nor addled by the societal norms dictated by chauvinism. You all are an inspiration to us. You give us the chance to hold on to a dream of a better future, a dream one day will be reality owing to your steadfastness.

I am eternally grateful to my daughter, Gabriella Nethari, for choosing me to be your mother. You are my muse, my source of courage. I am humbled by your wisdom, strength, independence, and most of all your kindness. You have grown to be a smart, beautiful, strong young woman who has defined her own existence. I love how you stand strong and continue to be true to yourself. Fly high and reach for the stars darling. Oh, and I hope you will publish your work one day. You are a talented writer as you already know. Share your talent with the world. I love you with all my heart.

p.s Just admit that you love me more than Cinnamon (cat) and we will be just grand.

To my husband, my other half, my perfect big Irishman, You are my NorthStar. I breathe easy knowing you are there. I'm not afraid to fall because I know you will never let me hit the ground. Thank you for your unwavering support, encouragement, and endless supply of tea. Now let's hit the brakes on bacon so we can travel the world together as we planned, shall we? I love you!

~"I wish I had met you sooner, just so that I could have loved you a little longer"~

To Tara and Conor, for reminding me of what I had forgotten; dream big, be fearless and that it's ok to push the boundaries. I am eternally thankful for your presence in my life.

Conor, we couldn't be prouder of the young man you are. Already a budding young entrepreneur. Great things await you. Many say you are a chip off the old block. I don't disagree. Just stay off the bacon, chips and a few other things and you will be just fine. :)

Tara, we admire your tenacity, your zest for life and love of adventure. Always remember who you are. Now you are proving to be a great mother. We will work on retaining your Irishness so Dad can stop singing Irish rebel songs. I love you both.

To Tim, for making Tara the happiest woman. Your dedication to your dream and discipline is remarkable. And you are simply a great dad. Keep it up. And remember to apply that dedication with the rambunctious O'Driscolls. You will do just fine. :)

To baby Lexi, our little ray of sunshine. World waits for you with open arms. You have brought us so much joy. I love you.

To my brother Dilum and my sister-in-law Emma, You two are my rock. The correct quote is "The blood of the covenant is thicker than the water of the womb." Emma, you are the living proof of that. You are the glue that holds us together. Now to the more commonly used phrase "Blood is thicker than water." Malli, (how we address younger brother in sinhala), you always have my back. You and I have built our lives on this very notion of family values instilled in us by our father. This is my pledge never to waiver.

To Andrew and Kaylee, so young so smart and so brave. I am in awe of your achievements. Andrew, our little Einstein, champion swimmer, pianist, the list goes on. You have the biggest heart. Kaylee, so full of life, sassy and intelligent. Your competitiveness will ensure you can be whatever you choose to be in life. You dance to your own tune and make the world that much more of an interesting place.

I am so so proud of you both. Continue to shine. I have no doubt that your names will be heard and celebrated.

To my mother, Thilaka, I owe my strength and courage to be who I am, to you. I often say that " I did it my way" by Frank Sinatra is the song that describes me most. But in retrospect that is what describes you. I guess I am your daughter after all. If I ever find myself in trouble, it is your DNA that will get me through the storm.

p.s. As long as she's standing, be weary of hurting me or my brother. Yes she is the law. :)

In the loving memory of my father Simeon, who I am is what you made me. My values, principles, thirst for knowledge and desire to be unconventional and different! It is all because of you. I owe my knowledge of English and love for the language to you. Although I didn't get your talent for music I must have inherited some of your language and creative skills. I owe this accomplishment to you.

To my friends, oh god, what would I be without you? Thank you for being a part of my life, my craziness and for all the wonderful colour you add to my world. Each one of you has been an integral part of my journey in life and a huge part of this book. Thank you! I love you all.

To my cousins Dinithi and Madhushi, we share a bond that transcends time and distance. Both of you have grown to be successful , tenacious women who aren't afraid to take chances. Walk off the beaten path. Perhaps it is in our DNA, The two of you are an inspiration to me.

Lastly but not the least, to my publishing team at the Lucky Book Publishing, Samantha and Simar! Your support and guidance are what made my dream a reality. When I was searching for a book publishing company, what attracted me to Lucky Book Publishing was the two young entrepreneurs, what they represented: two young women standing strong, believing in themselves and making a change. This book is not just a novel for me but a representation of struggles of real people, a voice to all those who fall victim to social pressures. Without you I wouldn't have been able to make that voice heard. So thank you from the bottom of my heart! I am privileged to have you on my team.

~ Nadee Fernando-O'Driscoll

LABYRINTH

Life is a labyrinth of dreams. Dreams you set as goals. A future in which you see yourself. As unpredictable life is, it takes you on a journey seldom on a straight road but often through winding and twisting paths with many dead ends. Thus, dreams you once dreamt are no longer apt. Sometimes they evolve, but at other times you discard the old dream, no longer relevant, and start completely anew. We walk through this labyrinth of life with dreams we dreamt and dreams we willed, some fulfilled, some incomplete. We drift through our dreams until we find the exit, where there are no more dreams to be dreamt.

TABLE OF CONTENTS

CHAPTER 1
Paradigm Shift

The sound of the crickets, full moon stoically contrasting in the dark cloudless sky; it was peaceful. Yet peace was anything but what Mala felt tonight. She usually loved the full moon, the chirping of crickets engulfed in stillness of the night. When the world was sleeping, she loved to sit in her favourite spot on the veranda, facing the hills of the tea estate in the distance, with a steaming cup of ginger tea, and savour the peace and quiet. It calmed her. She loved the fragrant smell of small, off-white Sepalika flowers with their orange stems. They bloomed at night and fell asleep when the world woke up. Mala had planted that Sepalika tree herself. She loved it. For some unexplained reason she felt a connection to that scent. Her mom used to say that perhaps she was a caterpillar that bloomed into a butterfly from a cocoon on a Sepalika tree, in her past life.

Her mom… Mala's heart contracted with pain. It had been 15 years since Mala lost her mom. She missed her mother, but the pain has dulled over time. Yet tonight, it felt like the day her mom finally closed her eyes after a few weeks of battling cancer. It was a shock to all of them when Sriya, Mala's mother, was diagnosed with stage four ovarian cancer. The doctors had given her six months. But as soon as Sriya found out that it was terminal she had given up. Mala had tried to get her to fight, wanting to believe they could win. But in the end she was gone within fourteen short weeks. Mala knew the end was coming, but it did not prepare her for the pain, the void, the hopelessness she felt when her mother finally passed. Her sons were young then. She and her husband were busy raising the kids and taking care of their careers. Somehow the pain eased over time. But tonight, it all came back. Pain raw and searing, tearing at her heart just like the day her mother died. It took over her whole body and soul.

She has been sitting in her usual chair on the veranda, God knows for how long, just staring into the night. Just like she did on any other beautiful, peaceful night, but tonight it was different. She was staring, not noticing anything. Not the moon, not the chirping of the crickets nor the familiar smell of her favourite Sepalikas, but simply staring into the dark feeling numb. Thoughts of her mother jolted her back to reality. Tonight, she didn't have her soothing cup of hot ginger tea. Instead, she was staring into nothingness with her laptop open on her lap. Her eyes fell back on her laptop screen. It has gone to sleep. Mala tried to think of her password. It was strange. She knew the password to her laptop, but suddenly she couldn't remember. She couldn't make sense of anything. It was DKlove0811, her sons' initials and birth months. She was sentimental. Oh God, how could she forget! Mala logged back in. Sakura Rosa-O'Keefe, read the Facebook profile. That was what she was looking at before drifting off to nothing land. Mala was looking at a black and white photograph on Sakura Rosa-O'Keefe's Facebook page. It was a picture of a little girl with a mischievous grin, with her doting parents on either side. It must be her first birthday; there was a cake, a barbie doll with one candle. Both parents looked happy and smiling. You could see the love in their eyes and the child, she looked so happy in the picture. She looked familiar. Her eyes and the grin reminded Mala of her youngest son. He looked like the child in the picture. Oh God, Mala held her breath… She looked like her!

"Nona, I brought you a cup of tea." Mala was startled. It was just Somawathi, her faithful servant bringing her a cup of tea. Soma, as they all lovingly called her, was like a second mother to her. She had been with them since she was ten, or was it even earlier? She is a gentle soul. She helped raise her two sons.

"Thank you, Soma," Mala mumbled, managing to muster a feeble smile.

"Nona, it is past midnight, is everything okay?" asked Soma.

"Yes, Soma, I just can't sleep, and I have some work I need to finish. You go to bed; I will lock up when I am done." Mala wanted to be alone. She saw Soma cast a worried glance at her as she went in.

Mala received an email that afternoon from Sakura, the woman in that Facebook profile. Mala didn't know her. But this stranger from 10,000 miles away had sent her an email that turned her world upside down. It changed everything....it changed who she was. No, no it didn't change her; it just added a missing piece of information. Like a missing piece of a puzzle that was now complete. Mala heard a little voice inside her head uttering words of reason. Yet completeness was not what Mala felt. She flipped back to the email.

The subject read: RE: Remembering Mrs. Helen Peiris. Sakura was a smart woman. She knew how to make sure that Mala didn't just delete the email. Mala felt irritated. Aunty Helen! She had a flashback to her "attained party," or "becoming a big girl," as it was commonly known. In Sri Lankan Culture, a girl is celebrated when she gets her first period. Much like how in many cultures in which a girl becomes a woman, being ready to be betrothed and bear children was celebrated. But now it is simply a tradition. A tradition slowly dying but that many still try to hold on to.

That was the last time Aunty Helen had visited her. Last time Mala saw her was when she paid a visit to thank Helen for helping enroll her two sons at Richmond college. Mala wanted to visit her, but Helen had not been able to make time. Mala found that a little odd, so she ended up meeting Helen at the school she taught at. Aunty Helen looked the same, just a little older. She had lost weight, but she always dressed well. Looked dignified. Yet Mala felt there was some sorrow in her eyes when she looked at her. But what was really strange was her scent. Aunty Helen must have changed her perfume. She remembered the scent. It was weird that she remembered it.

Later Mala sent a gift basket to which she added a bottle of Goya Jasmine perfume. It was the scent Mala associated with Aunty Helen. Mala liked Helen. Helen and her husband Peter used to visit her. She remembered most of those visits vividly. There was a familiarity about them. They came for all her birthdays up until she was 12. At least the ones she remembers. She remembered herself as a toddler, crying when they left after visiting and how it annoyed her father. He would say, "Mala, if you don't stop crying, they won't come to visit you again." She was just a toddler, and she was an only child. She enjoyed the attention. Then the visits stopped after her "becoming a big girl" party.

The human brain is quite remarkable. It has a lifetime of data in the form of memories, scents, sounds and even touch, all stored deep within. Sometimes so deep that they are almost forgotten. But just a whiff of a scent, a song , a word brings those memories flooding back. It's almost like your brain sometimes decides to hide those memories to protect you. It notices, takes stock of and stores everything, even the most insignificant information you didn't even realize you noticed. It keeps you waiting, biding its time, writing the story. And then there's the trigger, the go ahead it was waiting for. One day, that small piece of information, the missing piece of the puzzle you didn't know existed, finds its way. BAM, your brain grabs it, figures it all out and throws it out in a collage, pictures in the form of forgotten memories brought to surface. A story that makes sense. It's all new to you, but somehow you know it's true. It feels familiar like you've already heard it. You know that it is the story you were waiting to be told. The story of your beginning. And just like that, the life you lived, your beliefs, the very foundation of the life you built, changes, leading to a paradigm shift.

Tonight, it all came back to Mala, the memories, the familiarity, and something else. Mala felt a touch of fear creeping in. A feeling she remembered from almost 41 years ago. She remembered her mom and dad whispering in their bedroom. It sounded like her mother was crying. And she heard her dad say to her mom, "Look Sriya, we will tell them that they can't see her anymore."

"Don't worry, Mala is our daughter and nothing will change that."

Mala felt terrified. She was only 12. She laid awake on her bed long after her parents fell asleep, everything quiet except for the crickets. She could see the moon from her window. Tomorrow was going to be Poya, the full moon. Poya is the name given to the Lunar monthly Buddhist holiday in Sri Lanka, and most practicing buddhists spend the day in religious observances.

There were a few Sepalikas in a small glass of water beside her bed. Aunty Helen had given them to her when she and Uncle Peter came to her party a couple of days ago. The Sepalikas had withered but still managed to give a wonderful scent. It was so sweet, and the sound of the crickets were soothing. Then Mala fell asleep. When she woke up the next morning, she had forgotten about what she overheard and the fear she felt. She was just a 12-year-old girl, happy and content.

CHAPTER 2
The Email

Dear Mala,

I hope this email finds you well. Let me start by introducing myself. My name is Sakura Rosa-O'Keefe. I have a brother, Nevan Rosa. Our parents are the late Peter Rosa and Helen Peiris, whom you knew as Uncle Peter and Aunty Helen.

I have been wanting to contact you for a couple of years now. For many reasons, which I will explain in the email later, I had to wait. I wouldn't say for the right time, as the right time was the moment I found out about you. But we, my brother and I, did not have the freedom to make that choice until now. By now this email is probably starting to sound a little strange, so I will dive right into it.

A couple of years ago, my mother wrote me a letter (yup, a snail mail) in which she divulged that she gave birth to a daughter on June 01, 1973. She was forced to give that beautiful baby girl up for adoption to a wonderful couple: Mr. and Mrs. Anura and Sriya De Silva. They named the baby girl Mala De Silva. Yes, you guessed it, you are that baby girl. My sister. OUR SISTER. You have two biological siblings, me and our brother Nevan. Our parents, Peter and Helen, are your biological father and mother.

I know how shocking this is, and you are probably wondering if this is a hoax like the Nigerian prince scam emails. You may want to hit the delete button and send it to trash. But please, I beg you to read the email to the end. You can verify our information. Both me and my brother have public social media profiles. I invite you to check our Facebook and LinkedIn accounts. We are both well-established and have nothing to gain by scamming you. All we are hoping is for you to know the truth, to give you the right to decide what you want to do with this information.

To give you some insight into who me and my brother are:

I live in Ottawa, Canada. My husband is Gerard O'Keefe. I have an 18-year-old daughter and two step-children. I work for a well known company called GS Partners, an investment company. You can see my profile on the company website.

My brother lives in Dublin, Ireland. He is a surgeon at the Heart Institute. He is married with two beautiful children who are 12 & 14.

You will see many pictures of us with our mother, who you knew, on Facebook. So if you have any doubts as to who we are, this should help clear them.

When I read the letter from my mom, my first impression was that she had lost her mind completely. I thought she was creating some drama for attention. Unfortunately, she had a habit of doing that. Losing her husband, our dad, at a young age, both me and my brother living abroad, and her being alone in Sri Lanka along with the pain of giving up a child and much more did make her somewhat tough and tough to deal with. I digress a little here. Sorry! But as I said initially when I read the letter, I thought it was just crazy. So, I fully understand that if you are feeling that this is some sort of a hoax or nonsense, I assure you it is not. And should you choose to reach out to us we are fully prepared to do a DNA compatibility test to prove it.

My father had a very profound impact on our lives. He taught us that family is everything and the very foundation on which my brother and I built our lives, our families. We are extremely close. Finding out this truth about you, our sister, and what our parents did somewhat threw our lives into chaos. We felt like this foundation was shattered. We couldn't understand what made our father make such a decision. But in the end, that very foundation, the value of family, did help us cope and come to the realization that everyone makes mistakes. We will never know for sure why our dad did what he did, but we know for sure that the family values he instilled in us are real. The moment we found out, we wanted to find you, to reach out to you. Our hearts ached for a sister we didn't know existed until that point, and we grieved for over 50 years of love, sibling fights, arguments, and a bond denied to us all. We wanted to find you straight away and reach out to you. We had this somewhat childish expectation of a great reunion and everyone happily welcoming a new family member, taking trips together, our children bonding with two older cousin brothers lol yes we are very passionate. Hope I made you laugh a little. But we were not at liberty to do so.

You see, when Mom wrote the letter, she specifically said not to ask her anything about this. She mentioned that she just wanted to set the records straight in her dying years (well she was healthy as a horse when she wrote the letter and only 73!!!. You would laugh at this if you knew her character ☐). I believe she just wanted to find some solace, since it was something that tore at her heart, a secret that caused so much pain, so she wanted to try and unburden. We tried talking to her, but she wouldn't budge. She said she did not want to disrupt your life, that you had a good life and great parents and that she didn't want to cause you any pain. I do understand that. I also understand Sri Lankan society. It is very judgmental and can be very cruel. I grew up there. I have friends and family. So, I know information like this can have a phenomenal impact from a societal aspect. That aside, I also understand and agree with my mother's fears of how this will impact you as an individual. After 53 years for you, suddenly to be told by a stranger that you were adopted. And I am so so sorry for the pain this is causing you. Having said that, both my brother and I strongly believe that you have a right to know the truth. If the tables were turned, we would want to know the truth.

My mom was adamant about not disrupting your life. Plus, she said you had lost your mother and you are taking care of your father. Considering your parents kept this a secret we knew it would not be right to take that away from your father. Therefore, my brother and I accepted the fact that we needed to wait until your father passed away and for our mother to either decide to contact you or to pass away. So now you know the reason why we waited.

Mala, what I am hoping, what my brother is

hoping, is that this would be an opportunity for us to get to know each other. To get to know our sister, to make up for the lost time, for a happily ever after. This is our hope. Both our families, kids including, know this story. We sincerely hope that this will be a new beginning for all of us. Having said that, we are fully apprehensive about the impact of this news on you. You and you alone can and will decide the next step. Should you wish to keep this a secret we will fully respect that. If you don't wish to contact us or for us to contact you, we will respect that. But we hope you will reach out.

Once again, I am so sorry for the pain this news causes you. I wish you all the best in life and wish with all my heart that you will reach out to us, reply.

Take care,
Sakura.

. . . .

"Mala…" Ruwan, her husband, has come looking for her, wondering why she wasn't in bed yet. His voice snapped her out of the trance. She was so engulfed in the email, wrapped in her own emotions, that she had not heard him come.

"What are you doing up so late? It's past 2 a.m." He sounded a little annoyed that he had to get out of the bed. She looked at him, her face ashen, her eyes filled with emotions: fear, pain, anger, confusion.

"Mala? What's wrong?" Her husband looked worried. Mala couldn't speak.

CHAPTER 3
1972

Drip. Drip drip... Helen was standing near the sink in the chemistry lab with a pack of test tubes she was supposed to clean and put away. She had just finished lab. Final exams were finally over. Years of hard work putting her through Teachers College, and it was finally over. She was staring outside the window. There he was. Tall, dark and handsome. AND OLD!!! He was old and his hair was almost all grey.

Nevertheless, he was a good-looking man, very dignified. She shook her head. Padma, her best friend, was standing next to her with a tray full of clean beakers in her hand. She followed Helen's gaze and her lips tightened.

"Helen, we need to go now. He is there, you need to go talk to him now. I will come with you," Padma said, gesturing with her head towards where the man was standing with a group of students.

Helen looked at Padma and shook her head. "No, I need to do it myself. I will go now." Her eyes filled with tears. "Can you put these away for me? I will go now…"

"Of course and good luck!" said Padma as Helen dumped the test tubes on the tray.

Helen grabbed her bag and ran out of the lab. Padma stared at the disappearing figure of her friend with a worried look on her face. Then she looked over at the tall, dark man with grey hair, talking and laughing with a group of students under a mango tree. So carefree. He was handsome and very charming. He had a way with words and this uncanny ability to command respect. All the students loved him and adored him. But right now, as Padma stared at him, all she felt was anger. "Bastard!" she muttered and turned away.

Helen was running down the stairs. Campus was not so busy today. Most of the students had finished exams and gone home, but there were still few students on the grounds. She knew that there would be a couple of more days left for exams for some. Then the campus grounds would be a dead zone until the next year when it will be swarming with students again. Busy with laughter, friendly banter, debates, and everything youth brings. There will be a fresh batch of students coming in. Full of hopes and excitement, eager for new experiences. For almost everyone, this will be the first time they live on their own. In Sri Lanka, children don't leave home until they get married or start working, and that is only if work is far away from home. So, for most of the students, especially for women, this would be an experience both exciting and intimidating.

The freedom of being on their own is exhilarating. Even though they are adults, parents, and the society itself don't treat them as fully responsible adults until they are married. Sure, you are expected to hold a job as an adult, contribute to society, but these tasks should all fall within the boundaries of what parents approve of. This culture of control over their children is so intricate that it gets embedded in them, guilted into believing they are somehow less than perfect if they stray away from the norm, leaving them somewhat naïve. Dogmatisms upheld and heralded as great cultural values deny the youth and young adults an opportunity to be true to themselves, and for most, forces them to live a lie, ashamed of themselves, carrying the burden of secrets. This society and culture are slow to evolve, especially for the middle class.

Helen was out of breath when she reached the grounds. It was hot and balmy. Sun was scorching. Not unusual for this tropical island. Helen felt dizzy and knew it was not just the sun. She was feeling tired for a while. Helen squinted her eyes and looked over at the mango tree. There was no one there. She stopped and looked around. Where was he?

It had been a crazy couple of years. 1970 – 1971 was not a favorable year for the Sri Lankan youth. The uncertainty created by the Marxist insurgency affected the whole country. Many youth, especially university and college students, were impacted. Quite a few of her batchmates were involved in political activities of the JVP. With the government crackdown, some were thrown in jail, and some went missing. Everyone knew what that meant. It was sobering to walk into lecture halls and see the empty chairs, knowing that some were gone forever and some were lucky to have survived but with their lives altered forever. By 1972, the activism had been subdued, but the residual effects were still very much present. Especially in universities and colleges.

Helen's life had changed as well. She was not interested in politics. But nevertheless, the events of the Marxist uprising altered her path. Helen was a dreamer. Helen dreamt of a life of riches and success. And she was determined to make that dream come true. But she naively dreamt that it would be a man who will make her dreams come true. A knight in shining armor would build her a castle in which to reign.. Naïve, but perhaps not unusual for a girl. Helen was smart, and teachers loved her at school. She was carefree, full of laughter and naughty, a flirt who enjoyed the attention of boys. She wasn't a ravenous beauty but attractive enough. She didn't like being the second best. She openly flirted and enjoyed the attention, but that's as far as it went. "I'm not interested in having a boyfriend," she told her friends, that was until she met Peter.

She met Peter in her final year at Teachers College. He was a lecturer at the school. She had seen him before, but it was only in her final year she had the chance to meet him. She took one of his classes, and with the Marxist political activities dominating campus life, he got involved in the student council. Teachers were getting involved in student organizations to enhance student safety. Helen was the secretary of the student council. Peter was charismatic, easygoing and at the same time had a way of commanding respect. Peter was also a great singer. You could often hear him singing "Shantha me raa yame" by maestro Amaradeva or "Please Release Me" by Engelbert Humperdinck while playing the English mandolin. Students just adored him. Helen had felt an instant attraction.

Helen flirted with him openly and boldly. She wasn't exactly sure where this flirting would lead or even what she expected. She just liked the feeling. Peter was a lecturer, and it was certainly not acceptable for them to be more than a student and teacher. In fact, he would be fired if that line was crossed. Forbidden fruit tastes the sweetest. But for Helen, it was just harmless flirting. She was no stranger to flirting with boys, yet she felt different around Peter. Perhaps because he was a full-grown man instead of an immature young lad. She felt slightly uncertain around him. Her friends noticed this, and they also noticed when Peter's gaze lingered on Helen longer than usual. Helen vehemently denied any feelings but secretly very much enjoyed her friends' teasing about Peter. She looked forward to any opportunity to meet him. So, when Peter started dropping in on the weekend meetings for the student council, she was thrilled. Slowly but surely, the harmless flirting was turning into a flame within her. She was falling for Peter. Without even realizing it, Helen, at the age of 21, had fallen in love with a man 20 years her senior. A man of a different culture and religion. Helen knew that a relationship between them would never be accepted by her parents. On top of everything he was a lecturer at her college. She knew both would be in trouble for it. Yet Helen was reaching for the forbidden fruit.

That year, after a hiatus of two years due to the political uncertainties, Teachers Colleges across the country decided to reinstate their annual intercollege student conference in Jaffna. Helen was more than happy to volunteer. She knew Peter would be going. None of the other female students in the council wanted to go. On a cool September morning in 1972, Helen, accompanied by Sarath, president of the student council, Nimal, a fellow council member, and Mr. Peter Rosa, was on the early morning Jaffna-bound train. As she sat next to "Rosa Sir," Helen was giddy with excitement. A naïve young girl in love for the first time was going on a trip with the man of her dreams. A man she thought had no idea about how she felt. A man she barely knew. But in young Helen's heart, none of it had any bearing. All she felt was the excitement of being next to Peter, sitting so close to him, hairs on her neck standing as she felt his hand lightly brush against hers. She was taking the train headed to Jaffna without knowing that it was taking her on a journey that would alter the course of her life.

CHAPTER 4
Second Chance

I've waited so long for you to write me,

But just a memory's all that's left of you,

Send me the pillow that you dream on, so darling, I can dream on it, too,

So I can dream on it, too…

Peter was singing softly while strumming the tune of "Send me the pillow that you dream on" on his English mandolin. It was an original by Hank Locklin, but his favorite rendition was by Dean Martin. Peter loved country music. He was a great singer. Peter started singing when he was just a young lad at the church choir. Although Peter didn't go to church much in those days, he often sang those beautiful hymns of worship. They struck a chord with him. It was familiar, and there was a certain comfort in that.

Peter put his English mandolin down by the chair and got up. He was feeling a little restless as he looked at the envelope on his desk. It was from Anoma, the love of his life. The love that once got away. Peter and Anoma were neighbours and family friends. Her brother and Peter's elder brother were best friends. They went to Sunday mass together. Peter and Anoma were in the choir, and that's where their love blossomed.

Peter had just graduated university and Anoma was still in high school when they first felt something more than just friendship. Peter had his first teaching appointment at a school in Galle after graduating and was back home for Christmas. The church choir was practicing Christmas carols when Peter first noticed Anoma as a woman and not just a little girl in pigtails.

"Anoma, do you have a stomach ache? I heard you moan," teased Peter, making fun of Anoma's singing.

"Get lost. You are just jealous."

But nothing really happened. Peter was home only for a month and then he was going back to Galle. He had his plate full. Peter wanted to become a lecturer and was studying for his masters. Anoma was doing her A-Levels. She would be off to university soon. It was next July when they were back home for vacation, both as adults, that their love story began. Anoma was five years younger than Peter, and he was head over heels in love with her. Peter already knew this was who he wanted to spend the rest of his life with. Both were smart, had the same taste in music and were from similar backgrounds. Peter felt comfortable with her, and he knew exactly what the future held for him.

But life had other plans for them. While Peter was busy trying to establish his career, Anoma was a young woman living her student life on campus. They had gotten engaged a couple of years into their relationship. Anoma only had one more year in university, and they were planning to get married soon after she graduated. But they were in two different cities and only met during holidays. And then Anoma fell in love with Rajitha, one of her batchmates. Peter had felt the distance growing between them and hoped it was just his imagination. When Anoma called him just before her graduation and said that they needed to talk, Peter's heart sank. He knew what was coming next. Both their families were sad, but life went on. It doesn't stop for anything. Anoma married Rajitha and moved to England. Peter continued his journey to establish his career. He was heartbroken and somehow didn't care to put back the pieces. Peter was 39 and still single when he saw Anoma again.

Peter heard from his mother that Anoma's marriage hadn't worked out.

"I met Aunty Priya today," Alice, Peter's mom, said as she handed him a cup of tea.

"Oh yeah, how is she?" said Peter absentmindedly, without taking his eyes off the newspaper he was reading.

"Hanging in there, considering…"

Alice was waiting for Peter's response. But having gotten none, she continued.

"It's such a tragedy. They had high hopes for Anoma, such a waste."

Peter winced at the mention of Anoma. He was intrigued, what tragedy? What had happened to Anoma? But he didn't want to engage in this conversation with his mom. So, Peter pretended to ignore her, trusting in his mother's love of castigating Anoma to prolong her monologue.

"She was a fast one. I never quite liked her. I didn't want to interfere, and that's why I never said anything when you wanted to marry her."

Alice was trying hard to bring Peter into conversation.

"Didn't you use to say that we were a match made in heaven?" said Peter with a sarcastic grin.

"I was trying to be supportive. I thought you

were happy Peter! Besides, would you have listened to me if I had said otherwise?" said Alice with some indignation.

"That girl was a fast one, and it was scandalous enough when she broke up with you and ran off with that fellow. Poor Priya and Alan didn't come to church for weeks. And now this!"

"Ok Mom, it was a long time ago, and why are you bringing this all up now? What is this big tragedy you are mumbling about? "

Peter looked at his mom, putting down his newspaper.

"Anoma and her husband are getting a divorce!"

Peter froze. He wasn't sure what he was feeling. He wanted to know why, but he dared not ask his mother.

"Well, that's sad, hope they can work it out." He picked up his newspaper again.

"Aunty Priya said it was done. Anoma didn't even tell them what the reason was. Such a selfish girl, she only thinks about herself. Always did whatever she wanted, no regard for her parents," Alice continued. "Bringing shame to her family, poor Priya is beside herself. Alan is not doing too well either. "

"Mom, we don't know what happened in their marriage. You are already assigning blame without knowing anything."

"What do you mean I don't know anything?" Alice was provoked.

"Marriage is sacred; you don't just divorce when things get tough! Why make the vows if you don't intend to keep them? When you get married, you make a lifetime commitment, you keep working at it. That's what you do."

"That's what you did, Mom," thought Peter, but he dared not say it out loud.

Divorce was very uncommon, in fact unheard of at the time. Marriage vows read for better and for worse and back in the day people kept those vows. They settled into their respective roles and just accepted it as the final verdict. If a couple was unhappy in their marriage, men strayed and found their happiness in other women, alcohol, gambling or in one or more or all of them, while women for the most part devoted their lives to raising children and maintaining status quo. Divorce was unheard of. So, when Peter's mother told him that Anoma was divorced, he could hear a hint of victory in her words, born out of hatred for the woman who hurt her son. After Anoma broke up with Peter, the dynamics between the two families shifted. Once close friends now politely acknowledged each other and moved on.

Alice was still rambling on. But Peter wasn't listening anymore. He was looking at the newspaper, but his mind was elsewhere.

"No explanation, nothing, and she expects her parents to just go on like nothing has changed. Anoma shouldn't have come back..."

"What? Anoma is back?" Peter looked at his mom.

"Yes, she was at mass today."

Peter had stopped going to church after their breakup except for special events. It's now been a week since Peter found out that Anoma is newly single and back home. This news had brought an avalanche of memories. He wasn't ready for all the emotions those memories brought to surface. Anger, sadness, hope, and fear, in no particular order. Peter was overwhelmed. But over the week, everything else subsided, leaving a strong urge to see Anoma, leaving Peter hopeful. So, when the weekend arrived, all he wanted was to see her. Peter was hoping to run into Anoma when he went to Church that Sunday. And that he did.

After the mass, Peter walked over to Anoma to say hello. Even as he felt his mother's disapproving gaze on them, Peter couldn't help being drawn to Anoma. As Peter stood gazing into Anoma's dark brown eyes, he felt a familiar stirring in his heart.

"Hello there stranger," Peter was trying to act cool.

"Hey Peter, fancy running into you here," said Anoma with a hint of sarcasm, and they both laughed.

"God, she's beautiful," Peter thought.

"I hear that you are now a lecturer."

"Yup, ticked that one off the list."

"Congratulations, Peter, I am happy for you."

"Thanks Anoma, I'm sorry to hear about your marriage."

"Ah, that… Well, it is what it is," shrugged Anoma.

"Peter, can I meet you over a coffee sometime? I need to talk to you." There was a sense of uncertainty and also little trepidation as Anoma waited for an answer.

CHAPTER 5
Water Under the Bridge

"Wow this place hasn't changed much," said Anoma, as they sat at the small table in the Veranda of The Taprobane restaurant. They have spent many afternoons here, sipping coffee and eating fish buns.

"So what is it that you wanted to talk to me about?" Peter was anxious.

"Peter, I… look, I never got a chance to apologize for hurting you. I never meant any of this to happen. I am so, so sorry."

"It's water under the bridge, Anoma, you moved on, we both did."

"I don't know if I call it moving on Peter, I made a mistake. A huge mistake that hurt a lot of people," said Anoma with tears in her eyes.

Anoma had said that her marriage was a mistake. She got caught up in the moment, but it was Peter who she had really loved. It had always been him. At the end, Anoma's husband knew her heart was not in their marriage and that was the end of it. Peter felt oddly happy to hear that he was the reason for the demise of Anoma's marriage. But what did it mean for them? Anoma was going back to England. Plus, Peter was not a love stricken young man anymore. He was 39 and mature. He was not ready to trust anyone anytime soon, especially not when it comes to matters of the heart.

At the end of Anoma's two-week vacation, she had gone back to London. But a week later Anoma had sent him a postcard saying that she missed him. After that they continued to write to each other. Peter felt the old familiar sensation of love creeping back into his heart. In April of 1970 during Sinhala and Tamil New Year holidays, Peter had gone to visit Anoma in London, this time determined to make her his wife. Anoma was elated. This was her second chance, their second chance! They both loved each other and together they were going to make it work.

It has not been an easy task convincing Peter's family to accept Anoma. She is a divorcee. In 70s Sri Lanka, a divorce woman was not welcomed with open arms as a new bride. On top of that Peter's mother hated Anoma for hurting her son. It was an uphill battle. In the end, Alice, Peter's mother, had accepted their relationship. Well, she really didn't have a choice. She knew Peter's mind was set and deep down she knew Anoma made him happy. Alice had seen how devastated Peter was when Anoma left. She had brought a few marriage proposals and Peter was furious. He had not even entertained the idea of humouring his mother's attempts to find him a bride, not even once. Then Alice had tried to subtly introduce him to other young women at family functions, but Peter was not the least interested. Alice was beginning to think her son would never get married. But now at 40, the woman that broke her son's heart was back in his life, and Peter is happy. Alice could see that. It had taken almost a year, but Alice finally gave her blessings, and Peter's family was ready to welcome Anoma back into their folds. Everyone was happy.

So then why was Peter feeling restless? The letter on his desk was from Anoma, saying she had given her resignation at work, and that she will be back home for Christmas. She was coming back to him. This time for good. They had once lost each other, but life had given them a second chance. They have won Peter's family over. Everything was good. Life was good, and they knew exactly how this story would end. It is a happy ending, their happy ending. Anoma and Peter would be getting married in August of 1973, in less than a year. Peter finally had everything he wanted. A successful career, a woman he loved and a future that held everything he ever wanted. Yet tonight, Peter was feeling restless. In fact, he had been feeling unsettled for a while now.

Peter knew the reason for this feeling but did not want to acknowledge it. It's stupid, she's just another naïve young flirt that will be gone soon. But even as Peter thought that, he knew there was something more. He looked at a paper with the list of names of students going to the Conference in Jaffna. Nimal, Sarath and Helen. Oh Jesus, that damn girl. Peter was annoyed.

CHAPTER 6
Yal Devi (Queen of Jaffna)

"Excuse me sir, sir. Sir, excuse me."

Peter felt a gentle tap on his shoulder. He had dozed off. It had been a few hours since he boarded the train to Jaffna, "Yal Devi," with three of his students. The gentle rocking of the carriages as the train sped through cities, towns and villages had lulled him to a deep sleep.

"Can I see your tickets please?"

The train conductor woke him up. Peter straightened himself and felt Helen move next to him. Helen too had fallen asleep with her head resting on his shoulder. Peter moved her head gently as he reached into his shirt pocket and pulled out the train tickets.

"Here you go."

"Thank you, sir," said the conductor as he returned the tickets to Peter.

Nimal and Sarath were fast asleep. So was Helen, now leaning her head on the windowpane.

She looks like a child, thought Peter as he looked at Helen.

There was that restless feeling again! Peter got up and decided to stretch his legs.

Peter stopped at the open door of the train carriage. The train had picked up speed. He stood at the door, sticking his head out to look back at the rest of the train winding through the lush green landscape adorned by paddy fields and tall trees with an occasional house in the distance, creating the effect of a motion picture. It was a warm day but the wind made it bearable.

"Sir."

Peter was startled. "Helen! what are you doing here?"

"We are having breakfast; I came to see if you want anything."

"Ah, thanks, Helen, yes I can use a good cup of tea, let's go."

Peter and Helen returned to their seats. Helen had packed sandwiches and a couple of flasks of tea.

"Helen, you think of everything." said Nimal while devouring a sandwich.

Helen gathered up the plates and cups once everyone finished their breakfast and took them to the washroom to clean.

Peter pulled out a newspaper and started reading.

"Oh, do you ever read a Sinhalese newspaper, sir? " Helen was back.

"I read both Sinhala and English."

"Oh, common sir, the British are gone, but still people like you worship them," continued Helen.

She liked provoking Peter. Especially in the subject of "his British slave mentality," as she put it.

"You sing English songs, you have adopted the religion forced on Sinhalese by them, and you love your English books," taunted Helen.

"First of all, Helen, music is universal. I sing both English and Sinhala songs. I even enjoy Hindi songs even though I am not well versed in the language. As for religion, yes, Christianity was introduced by the Portuguese, the Dutch and the British, not always righteously. Buddhism was not introduced in Sri Lanka until the 3rd century BCE. Once the King converted,his people followed."

Helen was thinking of a comeback, but she couldn't find one. She always felt unsettled around him.

"Fundamentally all religions teach the same values; it is unfortunate that people spend so much time arguing that their religion is better than the other, creating all this friction which contradicts the very principles of religion."

Helen was pouting and Peter was enjoying it.

And one should never limit themselves when it comes to knowledge. There is a lot you can learn if you open your mind and let go of the bigotry. Learning another language is not something to be ashamed of. In fact, I know Paali and Sanskrit as well." Peter sat back with a satisfied grin.

Helen, feeling defeated, continued to pout.

"Helen, you are wearing a dress, a fashion choice passed down by the colonists, shouldn't you be wearing a saree?" piped in Sarath with a grin.

"A dress is more practical in this warm weather, Sarath, and being patriotic doesn't mean you must be uncomfortable."

She was annoyed. Did Rosa Sir just call her a bigot? She didn't like being defeated. She must have the last word. But she was defeated. In fact, she had been feeling defeated ever since she met Rosa Sir. He made her feel foolish and Helen was not impressed.

There was always a certain coldness in the way he interacted with her. What infuriated her even more was that Peter was quite friendly with other students. Peter often joked with them and had a very lighthearted temperament. But not with Helen. He almost ignored her unless it was a matter of studies or Helen spoke to him directly. Helen did not like that at all. She wanted to be the center of attention, and being ignored like this was not sitting well with her. So, in typical Helen style, she targeted Peter with her sarcasm and constantly made comments about his "English-loving mentality."

While Helen thought Peter was indifferent to her, it was quite the opposite. Peter noticed Helen the very first day she sat in his class. He noticed the flirtatious young woman, full of life and laughter, and was instantly drawn to her. She was bright and so full of life. He was old enough to recognize that she was flirting with him. Perhaps she quite didn't realize that. What unsettled Peter was not that he enjoyed the attention, but that Helen's immature childish nonsense behavior was alluring to him. Like a drug that he was getting addicted to.

It was late in the night when they finally reached their destination. The next few days flew by. The conference was a success. Peter met a couple of his old friends from university, Velu and Rajan. They met for drinks in the night at the teachers' quarters where they were staying. Helen, Nimal and Sarath were staying in the student dormitories. Peter was relaxed, strumming a tune on his English mandolin while his friends enjoyed a bottle of arrack, the Sri Lankan whisky. Peter was a teetotaler. He had seen what alcohol did to his father and the suffering his mother went through. Peter swore that he will never touch alcohol. They talked about old days, and Peter told his friend that he and Anoma got back together. Peter told them to keep next August free to attend his wedding.

It was time to go back. Peter was at the train station with Nimal, Sarath and Helen. There was a certain uncertainty in the air that day. A sense of foreboding passed through them as they listened to the announcement on the loudspeaker. There had been some unrest the night before. They weren't quite sure what had happened, but the train to Colombo was canceled. There were whispers about an attack by insurgents and curfew in certain areas. Peter's friend Velu was driving to Trinco and offered to drive them there. The next day, they would have to take a bus to Colombo.

They were all tense. Peter was worried, as he was responsible for the safety of Nimal, Sarath and Helen.

It was not a favourable time to be stranded with three young people. Especially Nimal and Sarath, being young men. Peter could see the concern on their faces.

Nimal, Sarath and Helen all filed into the back of Velu's car with Peter at the front. The car rolled through the unusually empty roads. There were military personnel every few kilometers. Conversation was subdued in the car. When they came to the first checkpoint, the guards wanted them to get off while they checked the car. The guards took Nimal and Sarath away from the rest.

This was when Helen first noticed how authoritative Peter could be. Peter watched patiently for a few minutes while the guards were speaking to the boys. But as soon as they started frisking, Peter's demeanor changed. Helen watched with a mixture of fear and awe at how Peter quickly walked towards the guards with his shoulders back, his jaw set and looking rather formidable. There was a certain aura about him; he was emanating authority without even saying a word. Seeing Peter walk towards where Nimal and Sarath were being searched, another guard walked in front of Peter with his rifle drawn. Velu and Helen held their breath while watching Peter talk to the guard and walk into the temporary hut set up at the guard post. Peter came out with a different soldier this time looking much relaxed.

"Give this pass to guards and if they stop you, this will get you through. Sorry for the trouble, sir," said the soldier, handing a piece of paper to Peter.

"No problem and thank you," replied Peter.

The soldier went over to where guards were holding Nimal and Sarath. Helen, Velu and Peter watched on intently while Nimal and Sarath gathered their identity cards. They looked rattled but relieved as they walked towards the car.

"Alright, let's get out of here," said Velu as he started the engine.

Peter looked at Nimal, Sarath and Helen in the back in the mirror. All of them looked tense.

"It's all good now. Don't worry," said Peter.

Nimal and Sarath nodded.

"Thanks, sir," said Nimal softly.

"Do you know the fellow back there?" asked Velu.

"No." Peter shook his head. "I called Frank from the post. He arranged transport from Trinco to Colombo tomorrow. It's all good."

Frank was Peter's cousin and a Colonel in the Sri Lankan army. Some rebel groups had attempted attacks on police stations north of Trincomalee and a few to the south.

"The government has declared a curfew overnight. But don't worry, Frank arranged an army vehicle for us to get home."

"Velu, are you sure we can stay with you tonight?"

"Yes, yes, it is safer. Amma and Appa have gone to visit my sister. There are three rooms. Helen can take one room, the boys can take the other and you are stuck with me, mate. Just like old times," said Velu with a chuckle, trying to lighten the mood.

Peter nodded his head. He glanced at Helen's reflection in the rearview mirror. She looked so frightened. Her eyes were huge with fear. The usual twinkle and laughter in her eyes was gone. She looked scared and vulnerable. Peter wanted to take her in his arms and hold her. He wanted to tell her it's okay and that she needn't be scared.

Velu's voice interrupted Peter's thoughts. "We'll be home in a couple of hours."

No one was in the mood for conversation. Each of them was lost in their thoughts. Velu turned the radio on as the car rolled through the winding road. Roads were empty except for the occasional vehicle speeding past and the stray dogs carelessly dragging their skeletal bodies along the side of the road. Dark clouds were gathering in the sky, casting a rather ominous shadow over the landscape as well as the five travelers in Velu's orange Volkswagen.

CHAPTER 7
In the Eye of the Storm

"We are here," said Velu as he pulled the car in front of his parents' house.

Peter looked at the familiar house with whitewashed walls, a red tiled roof and a wrap-around veranda. He had spent many weekends here visiting Velu. Fond memories of their youth spent here while Velu's mother fussed over them with an endless supply of vada (the fried donut-shaped savory snack made of ground legumes) and tea came flooding back. It was nice to be back here, in the safety of familiar grounds.

Rain was pouring down mercilessly. The house was completely dark.

"Shit, no electricity," said Velu after fumbling with the switches.

"There might have been a power surge with the

lightning. I will go check the breakers," said Velu as he lit a candle.

"Nimal and Sarath, you will have to take my office room. I don't have an extra bed, but I have a couple of sleeping mats in there."

"That's plenty, Velu sir, we are very grateful."

"No problem, son."

"Helen, this is your room," said Velu, opening a door next to the kitchen.

"Thank you," muttered Helen.

"Alrighty, I will see what we can rustle up for dinner. I'm starving," said Peter.

"We are out of luck, guys, there seems to be a power outage. The lightning might have struck a transformer." Velu was back from checking the breakers.

"Few drinks and a nice bite, that's all I need. I know I will sleep like a baby, Velu sir," said Nimal, pulling out a bottle of Arrack.

"You shouldn't be drinking with the teachers," said Helen with a disapproving look.

"Ah, I think we can make an exception Helen, It was a tough day," said Velu diplomatically.

"Have a drink, Helen. It will help you have some

fun," teased Sarath.

"I don't need to drink that disgusting thing to have fun. I'm not weak like you guys." Old Helen was back.

Peter looked over and smiled. He was happy to see that Helen was back to her usual self. In fact, everyone seemed to be relaxing. They were all relieved that they were safe, and the worries of the day were behind them.

"I will cook," said Helen to Peter and Velu as she walked into the kitchen.

"Thank you, Helen. We will help you."

"Aiyoo sir, I like to eat my food, so leave it to the expert."

"Kitchen is all yours then, Helen," Velu laughed and went to join Nimal and Sarath.

Peter stayed with Helen. He was looking at her, and she looked different. Or was he seeing her differently tonight? Helen's hair was still wet from the shower and was in a loose braid. She was busy chopping onion and garlic to make a dhal curry. The onions were irritating her eyes. Helen absentmindedly wiped her eyes with the back of her hand. The glow of the candlelight illuminated her face. She was beautiful. Peter stood there mesmerized, staring at her, unable to move.

Helen could feel his gaze on her. She felt a little unsteady and excited at the same time.

"Can you get me a lime from the basket over there, sir?"

"Of course."

Why is he looking at me like that? Helen's mind was busy. For the first time since she met Peter, he was noticing her. It made her happy. Helen felt very self-aware. Her heart was racing just a little bit. Something had changed, and she liked that change.

"Let me help you, Helen." Peter took a knife and cut the lime in half.

He playfully squeezed half a lime at Helen and she squealed.

"What's going on back there? Are you cooking or having a circus?" Nimal got up and walked over.

"Rosa Sir, how about a little music?" he said, picking up Peter's English Mandolin.

"Alright, alright, I'm coming." Peter looked at Helen for a minute and tucked a strand of loose hair behind her ear, lightly caressing her face as he turned and left to join the men. Helen stood there frozen. She could hear her heart beating loud, so loud that she was sure others could hear it too. How could a mere glance, a gentle touch from this man make her feel so giddy? Earlier today Helen's heart was pounding so loud out of fear. She was scared for her friends and for herself. She wanted nothing more than to be home with her parents and her sisters. And now, just a few hours later, Helen's heart was pounding loud again but this time it was with happiness. And all she wanted was to be here, with Peter in this moment, forever!

"Helen, do you think we could have dinner tonight?" shouted Sarath from the sofa, breaking Helen's trance.

"It will be ready in half an hour!" shouted Helen back.

Two hours later Nimal, Sarath, Velu, Peter and Helen all sat in Velu's living room singing around the coffee table. Laughter and playful banter filled the candle lit room in stark contrast to the fear and deafening silence that surrounded them earlier in the day.

"Oh island in the sun, built for me by my father's hand..." Peter carried on.

Nimal and Sarath were dozing off and so was Velu. They had polished off the bottle of Arrack and were feeling tired. It has been a long day.

"Ok lads, I'm going to bed," said Velu, finally pulling himself up.

"Me too," Sarath got up, and Nimal followed suit.

Peter and Helen didn't move.

"Are you coming?" Velu looked at Peter quizzically.

"You go on, I need to unwind a little," said Peter without looking at him.

Velu looked at Helen but didn't say anything. He had picked up on the charged air between the two. But he knew Peter well enough. Peter was not the type to make any reckless mistakes. Helen was a student and Peter her teacher. He would surely not risk his career for this naïve young woman. Then there was Anoma, the love of Peter's life. Velu knew how much Peter loved Anoma, and they were getting married next year. Surely Peter would not do anything to jeopardize that. Not after all these years of waiting. But Velu wasn't so sure. There was just something about these two that didn't give Velu the reassurance he was seeking. He lingered for a minute then shook his head and turned around.

"Ok, I'm out then," said Velu as he headed towards his room.

Peter and Helen were finally alone in the room. The candle was casting figures on the walls as the flame danced to the soft wind blowing through the louvered windows. Rain was still pouring down relentlessly with occasional lightning immediately followed by the sound of thunder. Helen shivered.

"Are you cold?" asked Peter.

"No, I'm fine." Helen didn't look at Peter.

They just sat in the dark living room illuminated by a candle and occasional lightning. The air was charged, and both felt it. Both knew deep down that what was going to happen was inevitable but neither one thought about it consciously. There was an unseen force driving them towards a road neither had planned to take. Helen was sitting on a chair opposite Peter. But both could feel each other's presence, almost as if they were touching. Peter was looking directly at Helen, trying to weigh the situation. His brain was telling him to go to bed.

This is a risky game, you old fool, his mind whispered.

"Anoma, I love Anoma." Peter got up abruptly.

"Goodnight, Helen. I'm going to bed."

Just then there was lightning and booming thunder, and a gush of cold air blew through the window, knocking the candle holder down.

Helen jumped, startled, and reached out to Peter. Peter pulled her into his arms and cradled her.

Helen started softly crying. She wasn't scared and

wasn't sure why she was crying. She was overcome with emotions that she had no control over. At that moment, Helen was simply happy, and there was an excitement surging through her, taking over her body, numbing her mind until nothing mattered but the two of them and this moment. She felt overwhelmed as she took refuge in Peter's arms.

"Shhh, shhh… it's ok, nothing to be afraid of."Peter picked her up and carried her to the room. He lowered her gently to the bed, turned around and walked back to the door. But once Peter reached the door handle, he stopped. Blood rushed into his ears, his heart was pounding, drowning the voice of caution in his brain. He turned and looked at Helen, her silhouette against the flash of lightning outside. She was looking at him intently, unsure yet invitingly. He closed the door shut and walked over to her. The small voice in his head whispering words of caution was silenced. There were no more images of Anoma creeping into his mind. There was only Helen and the desire that was burning through him.

The heavens continued to release a torrent of rain amidst flashes of lightning and rolling thunder not unlike the deluge of passion that engulfed Helen and Peter. Casting aside all social norms, caution, commitments and their dreams, they gave in to the most primal carnal pleasure of life. And just like that, destiny overpowered the dreams of two individuals, altering the course of their future in a way neither could ever imagine.

55

CHAPTER 8
If I Could Turn Back Time

Peter and Helen lay in bed, spent and each lost in their own thoughts. Helen snuggled into Peter with her head resting on his bare chest. Happy and content, she did not want this night to end. This was where she belonged. She loved this man; he is her future. Helen was dreaming of getting married to Peter, her wedding saree: a white net saree with silver embroidery. "I will have a seven-tier cake". She smiled.

"I love you," whispered Helen as she drifted into a dreamless sleep.

Peter lay wide awake, cradling Helen with his left arm as she slept on his chest and resting his head on his right arm, fist clenched in a tight ball. He could hear the rain pitter patter on the window. The rain had diminished but stubbornly refused to let up. He could still hear the sound of occasional thunder in the distance.

Peter had heard Helen whisper, "I love you." He froze. He couldn't bring himself to say anything. While Helen was fast asleep content and happy, Peter lay still, filled with regret and self-loathing.

What the hell had he done?! Jesus, what was he going to tell Helen?

He couldn't breathe. He must get out of here. But Peter didn't want to wake Helen. He didn't have the strength to engage in conversation, and he didn't have the slightest idea what he was going to tell her. So, he lay there motionless, listening to the steady rain drops, engulfed in a torrent of emotions threatening to rob him of his sanity.

Finally, after about an hour or so which felt like an eternity, Peter slowly pulled himself up and gently tucked the covers over Helen. He pulled his pants on and quietly left the room. Guilt consumed him. This was Helen's first time. Jesus, of course it is, what was he thinking! She was a naïve, 22-year-old girl who has never left home for anything except to go to college.

The rain had stopped. Peter sat in Velu's dark living room in total silence. Except for the occasional croaking of bullfrogs in the puddles of water, there was not a peep. His head was throbbing. He leaned forward holding his head in his hands, massaging the pulsating temples. Nothing was easing the pain; nothing was going to fix this mess.

Perhaps it wouldn't be that bad. It was only two and a half months until Helen would graduate. She would be busy with coursework and exams once they got back, and then she would be gone. Gone from his life. Peter tried to reassure himself.

But Peter knew he was just fooling himself. Yet he didn't want to admit it.

What is done is done, he couldn't turn back time. He would play it cool until they got back. Perhaps he would take a week off. It would give Helen enough time to think about what she wanted. She possibly wouldn't want to do anything with him. She knew they were from two different worlds and had nothing in common, and he was 42, almost twenty bloody years older than her. He would be honest with her. She was an intelligent girl. Surely, she wouldn't want this one mistake to ruin her whole life.

Peter relaxed a little. He had a plan. Peter knew that time is a wonderful healer. Once Helen had time to think and calm down, she would see that last night was nothing more than a stupid mistake. If she was worried about her future, he knew of a hospital that performed reconstructive surgery. His cousin, a doctor there, had told him about girls who came there. Sometimes parents would bring them over to "correct a mistake" they made, so they can go on to live a happy life with a man they eventually marry, leaving no traces of the past other than somewhere in their memory, buried deep. Peter would pay for it of course. Helen wasn't the first one to lose her virginity for a night of passion. Peter tried to convince himself, suppressing his unease.

Peter took a deep breath, sat back and looked outside the window. First light of dawn was beginning to break through the horizon. Anoma didn't have to know. He made a mistake, for heaven's sake. He was allowed to make a mistake, was he not? After all, Anoma left him for another man. She did this to him once. Peter felt a surge of anger rising as he thought about Anoma's betrayal. Well, now they were equal. Peter was searching for justification. But he didn't want to acknowledge that. He was desperate.

Peter refused to acknowledge the guilt simmering in his gut and completely ignored how Helen might feel. With the sunrise, amidst the chirping of birds, Peter felt a modicum of hope. He needed that.

"Morning, Rosa." Velu was up. "Did you sleep on the sofa or elsewhere?"

There was a hint of anger mixed with sarcasm in Velu's voice. Peter didn't respond. He didn't want to lie to Velu, but he was in no mood for conversation. Least of all about where he slept last night. Velu started the stove, put the kettle on and came over to where Peter was. He stood looking at Peter for a few minutes and sat next to him with a sigh.

"You look like shit." Velu was waiting for Peter to say something, but when he didn't, Velu carried on. "Look man, you are an adult, and at the end of the day what you do is your business. But as your friend let me give you a piece of advice; this girl Helen, she is young and exciting, but man she couldn't be more different from you. This fling or whatever this is, it's not going to last. And I have known you all my adult life. You and Anoma have something real. I was there when she left you, and you were devastated. After all these years, she's back in your life, and I have never seen you happier. Don't throw that all away."

"I'm not losing Anoma again!" There was determination in Peter's voice. He leapt to his feet and walked outside. There was that knot in his stomach again. Fear mixed with guilt gripped his heart. He could feel the vein in his head throbbing. He cannot, he cannot lose Anoma. She was the love of his life, his future, his destiny. Helen was a mistake. It would never happen again.

"You could lose your job." Velu had followed him outside. Peter took a deep breath. The air was still damp from the rain but there was a certain freshness. It cleared his head a little. He ran his hand through his hair, sighed and turned to Velu, who had been by his side through thick and thin. It was his friends that got him through Anoma's betrayal. It was thanks to his friends that he didn't spiral down a dark hole of self-pity and alcohol. Peter understood Velu's concerns. He understood it so well, in fact, that Peter spent the whole damn night churning the same concerns in his head, repeatedly.

"Velu I know…it was a mistake, a goddamn foolish mistake. It will not happen again and I just need to get this day over with. Get them back to college safely and that's it. Just do me a favour, drop it, please?"

Velu started to speak but decided against it, patted Peter's shoulder, and went inside the house.

"Good morning Peter," Helen whispered, sneaking up behind him.

It sounded strange, unfamiliar on her lips, but calling him Peter was her rite of passage to acknowledging their newborn romance.

Helen was taken aback when she woke up in the empty bed, but soon it was replaced by a warm feeling. She had shared a wonderful night with the love of her life. Peter was gentle and strong. Helen touched the pillow Peter slept on, which still smelled like him. She buried her face in the pillow, inhaling his scent and hugged it tightly. She was happy and felt like a whole new person. She was no longer an innocent young girl but a woman. She had defied the norms of the society she belonged to, the values she was brought up with and the very notion of the virtue of purity a woman is expected to protect until she is married.

Helen felt a pang of guilt as she thought of her parents. This was not something they would ever approve of. It would be a scandal. Peter was old and a Christian and that's all she knew of him. What was his family like? Helen came from a Buddhist family with strong Sinhala nationalist ideologies. Her father was a principal at the local school, well-respected in the community and a pillar of the Buddhist temple in their small town. They will never approve of her marrying Peter. Helen sat up with a frown. Maybe she could convince Peter to convert. Her grandmother was a Christian but had become a Buddhist after she married her grandfather. She never spoke about her religion; she went to the temple with Helen's grandfather and celebrated Vesak not Christmas.

Did she have a choice? Helen's frown deepened. Would her grandfather have converted to Christianity for his wife? They were old fashioned, still checking for an auspicious time to step out of the house. They would just have to accept that she was not backward like them. Helen got to her feet and pulled her housecoat from the bag and wrapped herself in it. Where was Peter?

"Peter," she repeated softly and chuckled. "I guess I will still have to call him sir in class," she said to herself as she went looking for him.

Peter was startled. He was lost in his thoughts and didn't hear Helen come up behind him. He winced at her calling him by his name. Oh God, this was not going to be easy. Peter had heard Helen whisper "I love you" before she drifted off to sleep last night. He was hoping and praying that she was just caught up in the moment. But Peter knew better. A young girl like Helen, with her middle-class, conservative upbringing, didn't just sleep with a man and move on. Mistake or not, Peter knew in his gut that Helen believed she loved him.

Jesus, she was probably planning a wedding in her silly head. He sighed and turned around, taking a step back to put some distance between them. He forced a smile and said, "Good morning, Helen."

She was beaming. There was a twinkle in her eyes as she glanced at him with a shy smile. Usually, Helen was anything but shy, but it was not a usual morning for her.

"You look beautiful," he said genuinely. Helen

reached to touch him, but he gently caught her hand, held it with both his hands, just for a second, and released it. Helen was feeling giddy with happiness.

"Helen, listen, I am your lecturer, and we will both get into a lot of trouble if the school finds out about us. You will not be able to graduate, and I will lose my job. So, we have to be careful. We have to keep this a secret for now, ok? You understand me, right?" Peter looked at Helen probingly. Peter could be very persuasive. He knew he had to play his cards right. There was a lot at stake, and he could not let his moral compass determine their future. His future. Morality was highly overrated!

Helen nodded her head, and Peter took control. "Ok , the army jeep will be here in an hour. Let's go and get ready."

"I will bring you a cup of tea," said Helen with a coy smile and a wink.

"Jesus." Peter felt frustrated. She was not going to be easy to deal with.

CHAPTER 9
Back to Reality

Two hours later, Peter, Helen and the two young men piled into the official army van Peter's cousin had arranged for them. Peter got in the front with the driver, happy to put as much distance as he could between Helen and himself. He was acutely aware of Helen's gaze on him and purposely avoided any eye contact.

Just get them back to college and he could take a week off. It would give Helen enough time to think and come to her senses. Peter repeated the same thought in his head, trying to convince himself. But deep down he knew it would not just go away. He felt guilty. He knew what he had done was wrong on many levels. He knew sleeping with this young virgin of 22 years was wrong of him. Robbing a girl of her virtue when he knew he could not ever marry her was wrong. But he could not dwell on that. Every time his conscience stirred, scratching the surface of his moral compass, he felt suffocated. His insides were convulsing in throes of unpleasant feelings, guilt, fear and pain. So, he did what he could to survive: he refused to acknowledge the severity of his action, ignored the guilt, forced himself to focus on his plan and tried to believe that time will take care of it.

Helen sat in the back of the van, unusually quiet. Nimal and Sarath picked up on Helen's subdued nature and teased her about it. But she was not in the mood for conversation. When she woke up that morning her heart was full and bursting with joy, like a teenager discovering her first love, giddy and exuberant. Helen sensed a coldness in the way Peter reacted to her when she greeted him in the morning. Instead of offering a lover's embrace, he had pushed her away. But she thought it was because they needed to be discreet. After that she had tried to catch Peter's eyes all morning and steal a moment before they left Velu's place, but there was always someone or something he had to do. Was Peter avoiding her? No, not avoiding, just being careful. He was right, they could not let anyone find out or both would be expelled. Helen tried to reassure herself. Yet she couldn't ignore the unease bubbling inside her.

It was late in the night when they finally got back

to the college hostels. While the boys were dragging their suitcases to their rooms Helen lingered to talk to Peter. The girls' hostel was on the way to the teachers' quarters. Helen was sure that she and Peter could find a moment to steal a kiss. Instead, when Helen reached for his hand, Peter had gently squeezed hers and walked over to Nimal without even looking at her. Peter asked Nimal to help Helen with her bag and went inside the boys hostel with Sarath.

Helen was taken aback. He was avoiding her! Her heart sank, and tears were welling up in her eyes. And then she was angry. How dare he! She grabbed her bag from Nimal and stormed towards her hostel.

"Woah, what the hell? Wait up Helen, what's gotten into you?" Nimal ran after her.

Tears were streaming down Helen's cheeks, and she didn't want Nimal to see. So, she hurried inside the hostel without even turning back to thank Nimal. Helen ran upstairs and took a deep breath, wiping her tears dry. She didn't want her roommate Padma to see her like this. She wasn't ready to explain anything to Padma yet.

Helen wasn't sure herself of what was happening with Peter. He was just trying to keep this a secret, and they would both be in trouble if it gets out. Helen kept repeating feeble attempts at reassurance, but it just didn't feel right.

"Hey, you're back." Padma was hugging Helen with a bagful of chocolate biscuits in her hand. Padma was Helen's best friend and her roommate. They had only known each other for three years but it felt like a lifetime. They had spent countless hours of the last two and a half years sharing their dreams, secret desires and plans in this little room over chocolate biscuits and tea. Helen was glad to be here with Padma. She forgot her sadness momentarily and the reason for it.

That night, Padma and Helen sat near the window eating chocolate biscuits and sipping ginger tea while Helen recounted her trip to Jaffna and the ordeals encountered.

"You should have seen him, Padma, Rosa Sir was amazing; those soldiers were in awe of him, and he just has this way of making people listen to him." Helen was proudly describing how Peter handled the stressful encounter with the military. "If it wasn't for him, God knows what could have happened to the boys." Helen was beaming from ear to ear, stubbornly ignoring the bubble of sadness that threatened to engulf her courtesy of Peter. She omitted the part about her night of passion. Falling in love with someone was joyful news one would gladly share with her friend. But something was holding Helen back. There was an uncertainty about her and Peter's love, and Helen didn't know how to handle it.

The two friends stayed up chatting and catching up until midnight. Helen was happy not to think about her problem at least for now. But when they finally went to bed, Helen could no longer ignore it. Helen lay there staring out the window. She could hear Padma snoring softly on the other side of the room. Sleep was nowhere near Helen. Her mind has taken her back on a journey; she remembered the first time she met Peter. There was something about him, something different. She always felt slightly uncertain around him, felt giddy when he praised her in class. Helen had never felt like that before. She was in love with him from the moment she saw him.

A smile touched her lips. Then she remembered his touch, how he carried her to her room at Velu's house, the touch of his lips, sex. Helen felt warm and, without any warning, the sadness that was bubbling inside her took over. Tears flowed freely as she sobbed quietly into her pillow. The pain of rejection, loving someone who wasn't ready to love her back, was so overwhelming. How could she be such a fool? How could she let him do this to her? The fear she kept at bay finally breached her mind. She had slept with a man, she had slept with Peter, she was no longer a virgin! And the man that took her virginity was avoiding her. Did she make a mistake? Was he just using her? No, he wouldn't do that, she was just being paranoid. Helen was scared and sad, but she somehow knew that her fears weren't baseless.

She loved him, and he was everything to her, but he had not said he loves her, not even after they made love. The nagging truth at the back of her mind was now front and center. Exhausted, Helen finally drifted off to sleep.

This was not how Helen imagined her love story to begin. Instead of lulling herself to sleep, basking in happiness like a girl in love for the first time, she cried herself to sleep. Instead of announcing to the world that she was in love, screaming with joy, Helen silently sobbed into her pillow. Instead of sharing her happiness, her love, with her best friend, Helen kept that a secret, feeling uncertain and guilty. She couldn't tell her best friend that she was in love with a man she barely knew. Her best friend, the one she had shared everything with, her desires, her dreams. Instead of marrying a prince who was going to make all her dreams come true, she now must marry a man because she lost her virginity to him.

Peter sat on his bed hunched over, holding his head in his hands. He had seen Helen's face when he asked Nimal to help her with her bags. There was the pain of rejection. He knew that look only too well. Years ago, it was him who stood alone, holding a phone with that look on his face. He remembered that day well. When Anoma walked out on him, his whole world had fallen apart. But he was a man. The only scars left were in his heart, and time had healed them. But for Helen it was not just her heart that he broke. He took her virginity. Peter knew only too well how harsh this society was on women. It was not just the emotional scars that Helen must deal with. This same society that hails a man for being a stud is so quick to call a woman a slut, stubbornly ignoring that men need a slut to make him a stud. Peter didn't know much about Helen, but judging by the way she behaved, her immaturity and her lack of knowledge on current events, he was sure that she hailed from a conservative family.

He sighed and walked over to his desk where there was a framed photograph of Anoma. It was taken almost 20 years ago at her brother's wedding. She was very young and carefree. They both were. A lot had changed since then. Both of them had gone through so much and had come a full circle to a point where everything was good again. But now…no, there was no need to tell Anoma. It was a mistake, his mistake. Surely Helen would understand that what she felt was just infatuation. She wouldn't want to waste her life on someone who doesn't love her. She was immature but not stupid. He would give her time to settle down and come to her senses, and then he would talk to her.

CHAPTER 10
But I Can't Help Falling in Love With You

Peter left early the next morning to go home. He had left a note to the departmental head saying his mother was ill and he was needed at home. A lie, of course, but he hadn't realized that it was just the beginning of many. He had not been able to sleep at all and had a throbbing headache. Finally, he took a couple of disprin tablets before boarding the bus, hoping they would bring some relief. The cool morning air felt good as the bus rolled down familiar roads and Peter closed his eyes with a sigh, momentarily feeling a sense of calm.

"Good morning. Woah, what happened to you? Helen are you alright? You look like you have been crying." Padma was taken aback when she saw Helen in the morning.

"I couldn't sleep," Helen said without looking at Padma. Her eyes were puffed and her face swollen. There was no way she could have fooled anyone.

Padma shook her head. "You have been crying, Helen, what's going on?"

"Later, Padma, I will tell you later. But right now we are late for class and I need to talk to Rosa Sir."

"Rosa Sir? Helen, why do you need to talk to him? Helen…"

But Helen was not ready to talk to her friend or anyone yet. She had to talk to Peter. She *must* know what was going on here.

"I Will tell you later. Please, Padma, please. I need to get to class."

Padma was looking at her friend with a frown."Helen, did your flirting go a little too far? Did he hurt you?"

"What do you mean my flirting?" Helen was getting mad. "I didn't flirt with Peter."

"Peter? You are calling him Peter? So, something did happen." Padma was persistent as she ran behind Helen.

"Padma, please let it go…for now. I will tell you later, but first I need to talk to him."

Padma hesitated but sensed the panic in her friend's voice. Something was wrong, she knew, but right now her friend needed her to be by her side. Padma gently squeezed her friend's hand.

They went to the lecture hall where Peter was supposed to be teaching another class, but he wasn't there. There was another lecturer teaching the class. Helen and Padma went to the staff room but didn't see Peter there either. And the same lecturer taking Peter's class earlier had taken their class in the afternoon as well and told them that he will be filling in for Peter this week.

Padma asked where Rosa Sir was, but they were told he had a family emergency and went home. Padma looked at her friend and saw Helen's crestfallen face.

Once the lectures were done for the day, Helen and Padma went straight back to their room. They sat by the window as Helen filled her best friend in.

"You had sex with him?" Padma was shocked. "Helen, how could you be such a fool? You barely know him."

"I love him, Padma." Helen said softly looking at her friend through tears. "I really love him; I know I shouldn't have slept with him, but it just happened. There was so much going on earlier that day, I was scared, we all were. And Peter was there, he was there for all of us, he was strong and powerful. And it just happened. He was nice and gentle. I was sure he loved me."

"Was sure? What do you mean you were sure?" Padma was frowning again.

"When I told him I love him, he didn't say anything. I didn't really think much of it at the time but next morning he was very cold. Well, he said we needed to be discreet, you know, 'cause we will be in trouble if anyone finds out. Which made sense, but I didn't expect him to completely shut me out. He didn't even say goodnight to me, Padma." Helen started sobbing.

Padma hugged her friend, not knowing what else to do. Neither of them went down for dinner that night. They didn't particularly feel hungry. Later, Padma made tea and sat down near the window with a plate of chocolate biscuits.

"He will be back next week, Helen, and we will straighten this out. Surely, he knows that he must marry you now." Padma was trying to convince both of them.

Helen looked at her friend. "What if he doesn't love me?" She was exhausted from crying and that exhaustion somehow cleared her mind. "What if he doesn't love me, Padma? I know nothing about him, his family. I know people get married not knowing anything about each other. Our parents did and they seem happy."

Padma nodded and lowered her head with a sigh.

The two of them had spent many nights by this window, enjoying a cup of tea and sharing a plate of chocolate biscuits, discussing this same topic. And Helen had always been adamant that when she got married, it would be with someone she chose, someone she fell in love with.

Her parents had brought a marriage proposal to her last year: a son of her dad's friend. Helen's dad had been angry when Helen refused.

"He's from a wealthy family and he is educated... You are a fool, Helen," her dad had berated her. "You can have a comfortable future. And don't entertain these foolish ideas of having a boyfriend."

But Helen was defiant, arguing, "You are old fashioned, Dad. When I get married it will be to someone I love, and I chose."

Her dad had been angry and her mother had cried. "You learn to love the man you marry, Helen. I didn't know anything about your father before I married him," Helen's mother, a gentle woman, a devoted wife and a mother, had said through tears. But in the end, Helen stood her ground.

Helen meant what she said. She dreamt of falling in love with a man tall, educated, and wealthy. She wanted to choose the man she fell in love with and married. How naïve was she to think that the choice was entirely hers, that she had control of her heart. When she dreamt of her future husband, Peter was not what she had in her mind. He was old and very different from her. Yet it was with him she had fallen in love. Helen never thought that she would be spending her nights crying with her best friend instead of celebrating her first love. This was not how it was supposed to be.

Perhaps Padma was right. It will all work out. When Peter gets back, she would talk to him. They must get married.

It sounded more like a solution than a desire. Helen sighed. She closed her eyes and tried to think of her wedding day. She had always wanted a grand wedding ever since she was a little girl. She dreamt of herself as a beautiful bride, standing on the "poruwa," the traditional wedding platform adorned in white. She tried to picture Peter standing next to her, but she couldn't. Usually running wild, her imagination tonight was tempered by a sobering reality. At that moment she knew that her only option was to marry Peter. That week felt like an eternity. Helen went about her day. From class to lab and back to the room to sit by the window with Padma and talk about the same thing: what Helen should do now. "Get married as soon as he comes back." The conversation usually ended with the same resolution: to get married secretly as soon as he returned. Then once she graduates, they could have a celebration. No one would know and no one would get hurt. That was the plan and Helen held on to that. There was no room for doubt.

On Saturday, Padma asked Sarath to find out whether Rosa Sir was back. She needed help with math, she told Sarath. Helen and Padma had decided that Padma should be the one to find out, to avoid arousing any suspicions. Peter wasn't back on Saturday, and he wasn't back even by Sunday afternoon. Helen was panicking again. By 6 p.m., she was restless and angry. It was clear to her that Peter was avoiding her. Emergency or not, he could have at least called her. He knew what he did, and no decent man would have sex with a girl and just walk out. She would not let him treat her like this. Helen was angry and, despite Padma trying to stop her, marched right into the teachers' quarters and knocked on Peter's door.

The door opened and there he stood, six feet tall, dark and handsome. Helen felt a surge of happiness. But that was short lived. Peter came out of the room, closing the door behind him. He didn't look so happy to see her.

"You cannot be here, Helen," he whispered while pulling her into the hallway by her hand.

Helen's temper was rising again. "Where the hell were you Peter? You just disappeared right after we came back. And We need to talk!" Helen hissed.

"My mother was sick and I needed to go home. I didn't have time to tell anyone. It was an emergency," Peter lied easily.

"So you couldn't find a phone for a whole week? You can't just sleep with me and disappear!" Helen's voice was getting louder.

"Shh, Helen, keep your voice down. You know what will happen if the faculty finds out. You need to go now and we will talk tomorrow."

Helen folded her arms and looked at Peter defiantly. "I don't care what happens. We need to talk!"

"Helen, we will. I promise. But not now. It is late in the night and if anyone sees us, we will both be done, end of story. You will never graduate, and I will be fired. Please listen to me. Go back to your room now. I will meet you tomorrow, say seven at night? We will meet at the Green cabin and we will talk. I promise." Peter was pleading, and he looked worried.

Helen stood with her arms folded looking at him. "Ok, I will see you tomorrow at 7 p.m.." She softened a bit and reached out to take his hand, but he pulled back. Then he said good night without meeting her eyes and went back to his room. Tears welled up in Helen's eyes and she slowly turned back. She knew that her love was not returned. She knew she had made a huge mistake. But this was her life, her future, that he was taking for granted. She was ruined. So, there was no other alternative. Peter had to marry her. She wiped her tears as she walked into the night with a heavy heart.

CHAPTER 11
Fool's Paradise

Helen was up at the crack of dawn on Monday. She had had a very restless night. Sleepless, restless nights were common to her as of late. Her stomach was in a knot; she was anxious to meet Peter. But that was not for another 13 hours. And she had a full day of school. This was the last stretch; exams would begin in a few weeks and then lab before three years of hard work would finally pay off. Helen wouldn't usually worry too much about exams. She was a good student, and she was confident she would graduate. But all of that seemed trivial to her at this moment when Peter was holding all her cards for her future. Her future, her self-respect, her happiness, all hung in the balance ever since that fateful night she slept with him.

By 6:30 p.m., Helen was a nervous wreck. She had changed her dresses three times already, finally settling on a lime green floral mini dress. She was a good-looking young woman, and she knew that. But Helen really didn't see herself today as she stood looking at her reflection in the mirror.

"You look great, Helen, are you sure you don't want me to come with you?" Padma was worried about her friend.

Helen nodded. "I will be fine." She picked up her bag and walked out the room. Green Cabin was only about 20 minutes' walk from the hostel. The restaurant wasn't grand by any means. It was convenient and usually packed with students and staff during lunch. But at 7 p.m., it would be deserted. That's why Peter had picked it, thought Helen with sadness. He didn't want anyone to see them, and he probably didn't pick a far restaurant to make sure that she came alone. He was going to weasel out of this. Helen couldn't fool herself anymore. She made a huge mistake, but she was not a fool. She let her guard down and slept with a man she was in love with. She loved him, and if he didn't love her, he shouldn't have slept with her. The realization of the situation made Helen's resolution firm. She was not going to allow one mistake to jeopardize her whole future. Helen did not see any other way than him marrying her. She was on the edge, feeling both fearful and sad.

Peter had arrived at the restaurant by 6:45 p.m. He

wanted to calm his nerves. When Helen came knocking on his door last night, he realized that it wasn't going to be easy convincing her to let this go. He had seen her defiant look as she stood there. It disarmed him. Peter knew what he did was wrong. Christ, if someone had slept with his sister and abandoned her, he would kill him. He felt like a coward. He tried to pull himself together. There was no point in ruining all their lives over one mistake. This is what is best for all of them. Peter leaned back on the chair with a long sigh.

Helen saw Peter straight away as she entered the restaurant. He was sitting at the back in a dimly lit corner, trying to avoid being seen by anyone. Except for a smattering of patrons, it was quiet. The only noise came from a young girl sitting near the other corner, holding hands with a young man. It was obvious that they didn't want to be seen either but for very different reasons. Judging by how they were leaning towards each other almost in an embrace, holding hands and smiling through soft whispers, she knew immediately that they wanted to be left alone, lost in their happy world. For a very different reason than Peter.

Helen pulled the chair and sat down facing Peter. Her heart fluttered a little as she looked at him. She knew she loved him, there was no doubt about that. The anger she had felt was replaced with hope.

"Helen…" Peter started but words weren't coming

out easily. There she was looking at him, with a hopeful look in her eyes. Her long hair pulled back into a ponytail, face fresh and young, she was a beautiful woman. Helen was feisty, talkative and mischievous; that was how her friends described her. But this girl sitting in front of him tonight was a far cry from that. She still had a spark but looked unusually somber. And Peter knew very well that he was the reason for her somberness. He felt the guilt rearing its head again, pricking at his conscience.

"Do you want something to drink? Are you hungry?" Peter signaled to the server without waiting for Helen's reply.

"I'm not hungry. I just had dinner," lied Helen. She had only had a banana and a couple of biscuits the whole day. But she wasn't hungry.

"Two iced coffees and fish patties, please," Peter ordered for them, ignoring Helen.

"Final exams are coming up, are you all set? "Peter was trying to ease the tension.

"Yeah, I'm not too worried… not here to talk about exams." Helen didn't want to waste time beating around the bush. She waited a whole week and had no patience left.

"Helen, I know, and I am sorry that I left like that. I had to. But I think it was good…" trailed off Peter as they were interrupted by the server bringing their order. "Thanks," muttered both Peter and Helen together as they waited for the server to leave.

"Peter, you left without even saying bye, and you were back on Sunday but didn't even bother coming to see me. It felt like you were ignoring me. Are you?" Helen felt her anger rise.

"I thought it would be best to give you some space to think. I mean what happened between us was… unexpected. Peter was choosing his words carefully. He had rehearsed what he was going to say in his head again and again. But it wasn't playing out as he had planned.

Helen felt relieved. He wasn't ignoring her but giving her space. She was smiling when she looked at him.

"Well that's very considerate of you Peter, but I would rather have you invade my space than keep me in suspense," chuckled Helen.

"I'm sorry, Helen, I didn't mean to worry you, in fact I didn't mean any of this to happen. You are young, smart and…"

He trailed off. She was smiling with a twinkle in her brown eyes, looking intently at him. And beautiful, he thought but stopped himself. He didn't want to give her any kind of hope.

"...just starting your life and have your whole life ahead of you." It was harder than Peter imagined.

"I know that. And I know you're old. I can see your grey hair," teased Helen with a mischievous glint in her eyes. She felt at ease.. He was just worried. How silly she was. She felt the weight she had been carrying this whole week lifting.

"Age doesn't matter, Peter. I love you and that's all that matters, that we love each other." Helen reached over the table and took his hands in hers. But Peter pulled away and straightened himself, sitting back, his brows drawn together in a frown.

"Helen, what happened at Velu's house…we didn't plan for that. I didn't plan for that." Peter needed Helen to focus.

"I know we didn't plan it, Peter, but I wouldn't have slept with you if I didn't love you. Look, I know you are worried about the age and school and the rules, but I will be graduating in a couple of months. And come on, the age? My uncle is 15 years older than my aunt, and I can give you many examples. It's not uncommon," Helen rambled on. "This is silly. I get the school thing, but the age difference is not something you have to worry about."

"Helen, Helen…listen to me..You think that age is not an issue but I am 20 years older than you. By the time you are 40 I will be getting ready for my retirement."

"C'mon Peter…" Helen was shaking her head, getting frustrated.

"No, Helen, let me finish, you are not thinking straight. Age is not the only thing. We are different people, we come from very different backgrounds. What do you really know about me? I know you think none of it matters, but believe me, it does." Peter continued without waiting for Helen to answer. "Trust me when I say this, you don't want someone like me."

"People get married without really knowing each other, Peter, it happens all the time. Half my batch mates are going home after exams to meet some guy their parents proposed and will end up marrying them. And they have their whole life to find out about each other. It happens every day in this country".

"And what happens when they don't like what they find?" asked Peter. Helen didn't answer immediately. What Peter was telling her was exactly what she told her parents. And here she was, having the same exact conversation, except that the roles were reversed. Tables had turned, and she was sitting where her parents sat and Peter where she did. Helen shook her head.

"But Peter, the difference is we love each other; no

couple knows everything about each other. They learn as they go. As long as we love each other it will be fine."

Love, marriage, couple... Peter was getting impatient; Helen was holding on to a fool's paradise.

"Helen, what happened at Velu's...we had a rough day, we were both scared and vulnerable. It shouldn't have... I shouldn't have done that. And I am so, so sorry. I know you believe that you are in love with me, but it is not real. You think that, but soon you will realize you made a mistake." Peter knew it was a poor choice of words as soon as he said it.

"A mistake?" Helen snapped. "You think sleeping with you was a mistake? Who do you think I am? I didn't sleep with you because I was scared, Peter. So what are you saying? That you made a mistake?"

"It was a mistake on both our parts Helen, this feeling you have, what you think is love, will soon fade. It's not love. It's an infatuation. You will see. You cannot love someone you hardly know. You cannot throw your whole life away, destroy your future for one mistake." Peter was pleading.

"Peter, do you love me?" Helen knew the answer, but she had to hear him say it.

"I'm sorry, Helen." Peter looked at her as he spoke and saw the tears well up in her eyes. He felt like a real jerk. But he knew the harsh truth was better than leading her on.

He could drag this on for another couple of months, and once she graduates, Helen would likely get a job in a rural school for her first post as a teacher. And then they wouldn't see each other, and she would disappear for good. Peter had thought about that option, but it was a shitty thing to do. He knew he was being a jerk and hurting Helen now, but it was more honourable than leading her on.

"If you didn't love me, why did you sleep with me?" Tears were streaming down her face. Even though Helen expected this answer from Peter, it still hurt to hear him say it. She felt like her heart was being squeezed by a giant hand. "How could you do that? You took advantage of me, Peter. What am I supposed to do now? My whole life…" Helen couldn't breathe.

"Helen I wasn't taking advantage and we were both willing participants. I never said I loved you. Look, I know this is bad, and right now you are scared and feel betrayed." Peter knew how she felt. He remembered the pain but also knew it would pass. It was the best for both.

"I am feeling betrayed because you *did* betray me. I slept with you because I love you. And if you knew you didn't love me, then you shouldn't have. What am I going to do now? My whole life is ruined." Helen started sobbing, and Peter saw the other couple glance at them. The server was pretending to busy himself with cleaning, but Peter could tell that he was very much interested in the drama unfolding.

"I know this is not what you wanted to hear but I can't lie to you.. But you don't have to worry about your future. I know a doctor who does reconstruction surgery. It is a simple procedure and more common than you think. He can fix it and no one needs to know. No one will ever know."

"FIX IT?" Helen couldn't believe what she was hearing.

"The re-construction surgery will restore the hymen. No one will know," whispered Peter, conscious of the server pretending to clean the tables close to them.

"I know what it means. You say it is very common. So, I guess this is common practice to you then. Sleep with young girls and get your friend to fix them!" Helen was angry and didn't bother keeping her voice down. She didn't care who heard them.

With that, she got to her feet and left. She didn't exactly see where she was going through her tears, but she walked towards her hostel. When Helen turned into the road leading to the hostels, she suddenly realized that it was dark. The streetlights were out.

She felt scared and turned, half expecting to see Peter had followed her. But there was no one. He didn't even bother to make sure she got home safe. He didn't even care that much. Helen ran up to her room crying.

CHAPTER 12
Gamble

"What happened? Helen what did he say?" said Padma. …

But Helen didn't want to talk. Not now. She buried her face in her pillow and let the tears flow. She never knew that falling in love could hurt so much. That it was a gamble, and the stakes were so high. She once thought she was in love when she was fifteen. She had a crush on a boy, one of her neighbors. He didn't know how she felt and she never found out whether he had any interest. It was all in her head, and she agonized over it for about a month. Then they moved and that was it. Helen had always enjoyed the attention; she liked when boys whistled at her or joked. In fact, she loved provoking them. But that was as far as she went. She had not fallen in love with anyone, until now. And finally when she did, she had gambled everything: her heart, her virtue and her future.

The next couple of days were torture. But gradually it got better. Exams were due soon and Helen was busy with studies. It was the final run and no one had any time to waste. Helen was grateful for the distraction. She sat at the back in Peter's class for the next month and was glad when they finally wrapped up so she didn't have to see Peter again, so she said to Padma. But secretly she looked forward to his class. There was a flicker of hope in her heart that he would change his mind, that he was just being cautious and would soon realize that he can't live without her and come back to her. Usually, these thoughts dominated her mind in the night, when the day was done and she was finally in bed. She let her mind wander freely, allowing her dreams to be her wings and fly high. In her fantasy world there was a happy ending for her and Peter. Amidst the sadness that weighed on her heart, these fantasies brought her some comfort.

The final couple of weeks just flew by. Exams were finally over. There were only lab exams left and Helen wasn't worried about them at all. There was a chill in the morning air and it was a welcoming feeling. Helen sat by the window with her morning cup of tea. She was feeling queasy again that morning. In fact she had been feeling like this for a couple of weeks now. Exam stress, her broken heart, it had all taken a toll on her.

She had lost her appetite and felt nauseous most of the time. She had gotten through the exam week on a diet of mango pickles from the street vendor and a slice of plain white bread. That's all she seemed to be able to eat these days.

"Here, I brought some dhal curry and string hoppers for you." Padma was back from the canteen.

"Thanks." Helen straightened up, setting her half empty cup down by the food. "Was it busy down there?" Helen hadn't wanted to go down for breakfast with Padma. She was feeling tired and wanted to take it easy.

"Nah, pretty empty other than a few. Sarath said hi to you and wanted to know if we would join them to go to the beach on Saturday." Padma cast a cautious glance at Helen. They hadn't spoken about Peter since the beginning of exams, and Helen had insisted that she was fine. But Padma wasn't convinced. She knew her friend well and Helen had not been herself at all. She didn't want to push her but thought an afternoon at the beach with their friends would do her some good.

"Maybe" said Helen absentmindedly, sitting down to eat her breakfast. But she couldn't get herself to eat. The smell of the dhal curry was making her nauseous, and she ran to the bathroom.

"What's wrong Helen? Are you coming down with the flu? Or is it the pickles you have been eating this whole week?"

Helen looked ashen as she slowly walked to her bed and sat down. She closed her eyes, trying to think. Her period was late again. It was October 10, and her period should have come a few days ago.

"Oh god, oh no, please…" She felt the panic set in. She was usually never late. When she missed her first period she thought it was because of the stress. And then she forgot about it. She was late this month but she didn't really give it much thought. The stress of the exams and being busy with studying didn't leave much room for worry.

But now…the loss of appetite, queasiness, missing two periods… Helen felt her head spin. She felt like she was going to faint.

"Padma, I haven't gotten my period." Helen's eyes were huge with fear. Padma stood looking at her friend, trying to comprehend what she was trying to tell her. But it was clear, the signs were all there. They just didn't see them, didn't want to see them. Padma sat beside her friend and put her arms around Helen. Helen was shaking and was as cold as ice.

"It is probably the stress." The words didn't sound convincing at all. Padma was merely saying them, hoping that it was the case. But neither of them believed it. They both knew the most likely reason was that Helen was pregnant.

They managed to see a doctor in town that afternoon. Helen didn't want to go to the college medical office. The doctor confirmed what she already knew. The doctor was a young woman in her thirties. She was kind and friendly. She didn't ask Helen many questions but looked at both Helen and Padma with an understanding look. She had seen girls like this before, coming in to test for pregnancies, their eyes huge with fear, sitting tensely hoping that the doctor would say anything, anything else other than to confirm what they already knew. It broke her heart every time. Most of them had never heard of birth control. Even the few who had knowledge didn't know where to get it or have the courage to ask. It was left to men, and for the most part, men didn't care enough. Most young women had no idea how to protect themselves. They lived in a society where all talk about sex was taboo. Even at school sex education was skimmed over. Parents didn't talk to their kids about protection. It was expected for their daughters to be virgins until they got married. Even having a boyfriend was frowned upon and they all lived in denial. That is, until something like this happens.

The doctor had ordered a blood test and told Helen to come see her on Monday. Helen nodded and left. She felt strangely empty. Padma hailed a taxi for them, and both sat in silence all the way back to their hostel. As they walked side by side, Helen saw Peter walking towards the lecture halls with another lecturer. They were laughing animatedly.

"I have to tell him." Helen started walking towards Peter with Padma in tow. Helen could swear that Peter saw them before he turned and went inside the lecture hall. She was certain that he was avoiding her. Finally when she caught up with him, he was talking to a few of the lecturers and she couldn't say much. She waited patiently for a few minutes before she finally spoke up.

"Excuse me, Rosa Sir, I need to, uh we need to talk to you about the paper," she said, gesturing towards Padma.

"Exams are now done, girls. There's nothing to be done. Why don't you both relax and enjoy your time before labs?"

Peter didn't look at Helen and pretended to busy himself looking for something through his books.

"It's important and we must discuss it." Helen's voice was quivering a little, and the other lecturers looked at them with somewhat of a quizzical look. But

Helen couldn't care less. She felt her anger rising.

"Ok, how about 10:30 tomorrow morning? I will be at lecture hall A."

With that, Peter turned and went.

Helen was fuming as she walked back to her room with Padma. She felt rejected and it angered her. For a moment the uncertainty and the fear that loomed in her head since the realization of her pregnancy was forgotten. She was filled with anger and frustration. She had made a fool of herself allowing this old man to take advantage of her. A desire to take revenge, to tell the whole world what a lying, conniving old bastard Peter was consumed her, and she wanted to see him in pain. To see him suffer just like she was.

That night Helen lay in bed, exhausted, but sleep was nowhere near her. Padma hadn't said much except to ask if she wanted to eat something. Helen wasn't hungry at all, and Padma didn't push her.

Helen met Padma in the first year of university. They were roommates and became friends instantly. Over time they became more than friends, they were each other's confidants, shoulder to cry on, they became family. Padma was more reserved whereas Helen was feisty, bold and somewhat unconventional in her ideas. Padma admired Helen while Helen found Padma's dependable nature comforting. Tonight, more than ever, Helen appreciated how her friend stood by her and supported her. Padma hadn't said anything to her nor had questioned her but silently stood by her without judgment.

It was around 2 o'clock in the morning when Helen finally fell asleep, and she didn't wake up until 9a.m. Padma woke her up to remind her that she was supposed to meet Peter at 10:30.

Padma and Helen got to lecture hall A by 10:20 a.m. and Peter was already there. The lecture hall and corridors were empty except for a few students walking to the library or seeking out a lecturer for extra help. Helen walked into the empty lecture hall while Padma stayed behind near the door.

Helen's stomach was in a knot, and she was lightheaded. As Helen approached Peter, he was sitting at his desk and pulled out a piece of paper with an address and a phone number scribbled on it.

"I talked to another friend of mine. He's a doctor. We can go see him right after you finish the lab. Here, this is his address. They do the surgery at the hospital but don't keep any records."

Helen stared at him blankly, unable to understand what he was saying.

Seeing her look, Peter continued."Of course, Helen, I will come with you. I will be there to help you through it."

Then it dawned on her. He was talking about the reconstruction surgery. Helen laughed and cried at the same time. "Unless you can turn back time, this surgery is not going to change anything." Right now she wished she could. More than anything in the world she wished she could go back in time.

"Helen, we talked about this. There's no point in talking about what happened. You know there's no future for us." Peter was getting frustrated. He thought he had gotten through to Helen. Since their conversation at Green Cabin, she had not made any attempts to talk to him. He had thought finally that Helen realized they both made a mistake, that was until yesterday. When she came up to him and asked to talk to him, he thought it was about the procedure. He would have preferred if he could sweep the whole thing under the rug and never speak about it but he couldn't. He would be there for her through this; he owes her that much.

"I'm pregnant." Helen's voice was barely more than a whisper. She stood across the table looking down at Peter and saw blood drain from his face.

"What?" Peter wasn't sure he heard her correctly.

"I'm pregnant, Peter." This time Helen was loud and clear. She was crying but she wasn't uncertain anymore. "So your friend cannot fix my future anymore. I am pregnant and we need to get married." There, she said it. This was not the beginning she envisioned for herself, but this was how it was going to be. As she said it out loud, she realized that she still loved him. Perhaps this was what he needed, the push for him to overcome his fears and take the leap. A little ray of hope struggled to peek through the dark clouds.

"Are you sure?" He was looking at her with desperation. "Sometimes, people get confused, you know, the stress and everything."

"I'm sure, Peter, I went to the doctor yesterday," Helen said calmly. Seeing him scared like this made her feel sorry for him and her anger dissipated. She waited for him to say something, anything. But Peter just sat there quietly, his fists clenched, staring at her with a desperate look.

"I was late and was feeling nauseous. At first I thought it was the stress of the exams and us." She smiled feebly. Peter still didn't say anything. She sighed and continued. "But yesterday I started throwing up and it hit me that I missed my period, twice, so we went to see the doctor. And she confirmed…"

Peter suddenly got up and started pacing up and down the length of the blackboard. He was staring at his feet with his hand rubbing his forehead. Then he stopped and looked at her. "My friend, the doctor…he can help." He said it almost smiling, relief spreading across his face. "Yes I'm sure he knows what to do."

Helen wasn't sure what he was saying. "I have another appointment on Monday, with the doctor. Do you want to come?" she said cautiously.

"You went to the faculty doctor?" Peter looked aghast.

"No, no, I went to the clinic in the city…didn't want to risk anything," explained Helen . This wasn't the reaction she had expected from Peter, but then again, none of it was panning out as she expected, her great love story, her marriage and pregnancy. None of it.

"If you are sure you're pregnant, what's the point of seeing this doctor again?" Peter stopped pacing and stood opposite the table facing Helen. He was a good foot taller than her. She looked small and vulnerable and at the same time stubbornly defiant. He felt comfortable standing and staring down at her rather than being in his chair.

"I'm not sure, Peter, but the doctor wanted to see me. She did a blood test. Probably to confirm everything and I don't know… This is all new to me too." At least they were discussing the situation. Well, that's an improvement, thought Helen.

"Well, you go see this doctor if you want Helen, but I will talk to my friend. He's a good friend, a nice chap and experienced… He can recommend a clinic." There was a coldness in Peter's demeanor as he said it. It unsettled Helen.

"That's good, Peter, I'm glad your friend can help us. But we need to make plans before it's too late. I'm supposed to go home right after lab exams, that's next week. But I will postpone it for another week. We need to get married before I go home after graduation." Helen was nervous. But she was determined to push it. There was no more negotiation now, no more excuses. The only solution was to get married.

"Get an abortion!"

Her blood ran cold as she heard Peter's words. Helen just stood there, rooted to the spot.

"My friend can recommend a clinic or give you some pills and take care of it." Helen kept staring at Peter, his voice sounding distant through the ringing in her head, and she swayed a little as she leaned on the table to steady herself. Peter quickly came around the table and pulled her a chair and helped her on to it.

"Are you ok? Do you need a glass of water?" Helen shook her head. She couldn't find words. Did she hear him right? An abortion?

"I will not get an abortion, Peter." Finally when she spoke she was loud and clear. "This is not a mistake you can erase. You had sex with me and now I'm pregnant. I cannot face my parents like this. I cannot stay in the hostel much longer after the exams and you know that. We must get married before I go home." Helen was crying, but she was determined.

"And then what, Helen? We condemn our lives to eternal misery? One mistake and you are ready to throw your whole life away? Is that what you really want? A lifetime of unhappiness and regrets?" Peter felt his blood pressure rising. He was angry and no longer cared about who was right or wrong. She was crazy and naïve. What does she think their life will be like? Hating each other for the rest of their lives? He felt beads of sweat running down the back of his spine. He needed to get away. He stood up, gathering his books and haphazardly shoving them into his briefcase.

"I will talk to my friend. You take the time to think things through. See your doctor on Monday if you must. But don't kid yourself, Helen, there's no happy ending for us. There's no us here. We are two random people who got thrown into each other's lives by pure coincidence. We made a mistake. We are a mistake. The only way to correct this, the only way for us to have a happy future, is for you to get an abortion. Sooner the better."

With that, he left. He came face to face with Padma in the doorway, but he didn't acknowledge her.

CHAPTER 13
Do the Right Thing

Helen sat there listening to the echoes of Peter's receding footsteps in the empty hallway. She heard Padma, her dear friend, hurrying to her side. But Helen just sat in the chair opposite the table and kept staring at the blackboard, feeling empty. She wasn't crying anymore, and she wasn't angry. There was just this void. She felt bereft and just sat there immobilized. She felt a gentle squeeze on her shoulder, and Padma tugged at her hand. The two friends walked back to their room in silence.

Afterwards, Helen sat by the window gazing out at the campus grounds. There was a group of students huddled around under the mango tree. One of them was talking animatedly and others were laughing. They seemed so carefree. There was another couple of students hovering over a book, probably preparing for their next test.

"I made us tea." Her trance was broken by Padma, who had made tea and brought a plate of chocolate biscuits. "What happened, Helen? What did he say" asked Padma while sitting beside her with a cup of tea in her hand.

"He wants me to get an abortion." Helen winced as she said it. The words felt strange and unsettling. Helen looked at her friend, expecting to see shock. Instead, there was a look of knowing.

"Are you?"

Helen was taken aback by Padma's question. "Padma? No, absolutely not, and how could you think that?" Helen felt slightly irritated that her friend, her only confidant, would consider that. "It's like killing, murdering a baby, Padma, and no, I am not going to do it."

"Then what are you going to do, Helen? Judging by the way Rosa Sir left, I didn't think he wanted to marry you." Padma looked serious, and there was urgency in her tone.

"He has to. The only solution here is for us to get married. He may not want to right now, but he will come to his senses. He got me pregnant, and the right thing is for him to marry me." Helen couldn't see any other way. She knew by now he didn't love her. He was just flirting with her all along. But now she was pregnant and this was serious.

"Well, that's what you want Helen, but Rosa Sir made it clear to you that he is not interested. He could very well walk away and he already did, today! He is a man. If he gets fired from this college, he will find another job. But what do you think will happen to you?" Helen felt disarmed by Padma's words. Her friend was usually timid, never confrontational, and Helen was surprised by Padma's directness.

"I will talk to him again. This is his baby Padma, and it's not like doing a reconstruction surgery and pretending nothing ever happened. The right thing to do is for him to marry me. He cannot abandon me." Helen persisted.

"And you think that everyone always must agree with you, Helen? You never stop to think that other people may have a different opinion? You have always acted like everyone else should follow the standards you set."

Helen was shocked by her best friend's accusations. "Padma, I thought you were my friend."

"I am, Helen, and that's why I'm telling you this. You think the only solution is for the two of you to get married. But Rosa Sir has made it clear that he doesn't want to. Now regardless of what you think, he can walk away and abandon you and the baby. What do you really know about him? Perhaps he has a girlfriend or a wife! Helen, do the math, you are almost two months along. You don't have a lot of time to decide, and if you don't get an abortion and Sir walks out, what are you going to do?"

Helen didn't want to hear what Padma was saying. But she knew it was true, this was the reality of her situation. It hurt to hear that out aloud. What did she really know about him? She had never seen a wedding ring on his hand, but he could have a girlfriend. She just assumed that he was single. She thought of all the times they teased each other. It was almost always subtle on his part. Well, he was a teacher to be fair, and he couldn't have displayed his affection towards her in public or he might as well have handed in his resignation. Helen sighed.

"You have to consider all options," persisted Padma. But Helen stubbornly refused to think that Peter would completely abandon her. She couldn't. Considering that possibility meant she must either get an abortion or face the consequences alone. Both options really scared her.

Peter's head was pounding as he rushed out of the lecture hall. He had to get away; he needed to put as much distance as he could between Helen and himself.

"Damn you. Damn you ... for fuck's sake. What kind of a sick joke is this, God? " He felt hysterical. He ran up the stairs two at a time once he got to the teachers' quarters until he reached his room on the second floor. He was glad that he didn't run into anyone. Once he was inside his room, he sank into his bed completely out of breath.

Helen was pregnant, and he must convince her to get an abortion. Peter felt that he had no other choice. He wasn't going to throw away what he and Anoma had over this. Soon Anoma would be coming home for Christmas. Peter's heart ached with fear and pain.

He got up abruptly and threw some clothes into his bag and left. He needed to get away from the university. If he stayed, there was a chance that Helen would come looking for him. He couldn't handle that.

Peter wasn't sure where he was going when he left his room. Once he got to the bus station, he realized that he didn't want to go home either. His mom would want to talk about Anoma and Christmas plans. Peter was not in the mood for all that. He decided to go visit his friend Melvin, the doctor. Perhaps subconsciously, that was what he planned when he left. It had been two months since he slept with Helen. He needed to speak to Melvin and make arrangements for an abortion. Helen didn't have any time to waste.

Helen was up early on Saturday morning. She was starving. She had fallen asleep around four in the afternoon and had slept through the night. All she had eaten yesterday were a few chocolate biscuits. Padma had thought about waking up her friend for dinner but figured that she probably needed the rest more than food. Helen got dressed and decided to go for a walk and told Padma that she will meet her for breakfast at the canteen in an hour.

Mornings these days were a little chilly and the air was crisp. Helen walked towards the mango tree and sat down on one of the benches there, enjoying the freshness of the morning. She was emotionally and physically drained. Padma's words rang in her mind: "What if Peter has a girlfriend, or worse, he's married? What if he completely washes his hands of it?" Still Helen couldn't get herself to think of the other option. Every time she thought of an abortion her blood ran cold. An hour later when she walked into the canteen, all their friends were there. The whole gang, Sarath, Nimal, Padma, Indu… Helen soon forgot her woes amidst the jokes and laughter. She needed that. She decided to go to the beach with them that afternoon. It was better than sitting alone and wallowing in self-pity.

It was late when they got back to their room. Padma hadn't pressed Helen about Peter the whole day. But once they were sitting down by the window as they did every night before bed, sipping a cup of tea, Padma broached the subject.

"I'm going to talk to him tomorrow, Padma. This is a baby we are talking about. His baby. He cannot in good conscience just abandon me." Padma sighed at Helen's words but didn't say anything.

Melvin looked at his friend stretched on an armchair in the veranda. When Peter came to see him, he was sweating profusely, had a headache and was out of breath. Peter had insisted it was the stress, but Melvin had checked him, and his blood pressure was through the charts. He was glad that Peter came to see him, even though the reason for the visit was not to get his blood pressure checked. He had prescribed medication and had given him a few tablets from his samples to last Peter a few days and advised him to follow up with his physician.

Melvin closed the door behind him as he came out with a drink in his hand to join his friend. He didn't want his wife to hear what they were discussing.

"How are you feeling?" asked Melvin as he pulled a chair next to Peter.

"Fantastic. Like I got hit by a train," smirked Peter. He hadn't lost his sense of sarcastic humour.

"You look it, too." Melvin retorted. "Is your

headache gone?"

"Better! Mel, I need this done." Peter couldn't get his mind off the pressing issue. The clock was ticking, and he needed his friend's help.

"Peter, I can recommend you a clinic, but you know this is illegal?" Melvin put his hand up when Peter started to speak. "Yes...yes, it happens every day and it can be done safely, but, this girl..what about her? You cannot make her do it, not unless she wants to. And let me be very clear, I am your friend, I am here for you, but I will not be a part of this unless this girl absolutely wants this. Man, her whole future could be ruined."

Peter sighed. Helen did not look as if she was sure of anything. And Peter had a distinct feeling that she would not agree to an abortion easily. She had looked shocked when he mentioned it and had not said anything when he left. Helen was a fighter, and it was very unusual of her to have sat there silently.

"I don't have an option Mel. What kind of a life will it be, for all of us? I don't love this girl. She might think that she loves me and hold on to this fantasy of everything working out, but she is naïve and has no idea how the world works."

"Yeah, but you do. C'mon mate." Melvin wasn't going to let Peter off the hook that easily. "You are a grown man. You are the one engaged to another woman. And this girl, she didn't do this to herself. You were a willing participant. So act like a grown man."

Melvin's words pierced through Peter. He felt ashamed and he knew he was acting like a jerk. He didn't need anyone reminding him of that.

"I made a mistake. One mistake. And all I'm trying to do is prevent another mistake. Marrying Helen would be a mistake, for all of us. I can't give her the life she's looking for. We will be two people who are condemned to a life sentence because we had sex once, once. We will be two people trapped in a marriage, hating each other. And that will not be a happy home for raising kids." Peter shook his head. "I can't do that."

He had seen it all before in his parents' lives. He was too young to remember much of it as his dad had died when he was only ten. But he remembered his mom crying and his dad coming home drunk. In fact, he had no memory of his dad ever sober, no memory of his parents as a happy couple. He had heard that his father used to hit his mom asking for money to pay for his gambling addiction, until one day when Peter's older brother had threatened to kick his ass if he lay so much as a finger on their mother. Since that day their father had done nothing but drink day and night until he died of cirrhosis. None of them talked about their dad with fondness. All he had seen in his mom's eyes were regret when she spoke of him. And it was not just them, Peter had seen that kind of family dynamic around him, people just living together bound by a marriage that neither party wanted. Women often bitched about their husbands and how they wasted their future. Men often sought comfort in alcohol or other women or both. To children growing up in these environments, it was the norm. Seldom they escaped the bitterness and regrets of broken dreams which their parents carried with them. They often ended up repeating the same mistakes, creating the ripple effect of a vicious cycle. Peter did not want that. Not for him, not for Helen and not for an unborn child.

Melvin sighed. He knew Peter was right. But unfortunately, right and wrong in these matters were not black or white. If they were in love the solution was rather simple. His friend was in love with another woman but got an innocent young girl who was in love with him pregnant. If this love triangle had any winners, it certainly was not this young girl. Helen's life had already changed, and it would leave a scar. She would carry that burden forever. All they could hope for was that she would be smart enough to play her cards right so that she wouldn't be damned forever. But he didn't know this girl, so all he could do was to hope for the best. He felt sorry for this girl he had never met. Melvin knew that Peter, being a man, could easily put this all behind him and live the life he chooses. Society was not so kind to women.

"There's an alternative option to surgery." Melvin spoke with deliberation. "There's a pill. But she must do it before 10 weeks. And any signs of prolonged bleeding or pain, you must take her to a hospital."

CHAPTER 14
I Have Loved Her All My Life

Helen flipped through her notes, simply going through the motions. She had an upcoming zoology lab exam on Monday followed by botany, physics and chemistry. It was a full week but she couldn't focus on books. Finally, she decided to go for a walk. Padma was lost among scattered lab journals and notes on her bed but asked Helen if she would like her to join.

"I'm ok," smiled Helen, seeing the relief on Padma's face. Helen knew Padma was just being supportive and would rather stay and study for the tests. Besides, she didn't particularly want conversation.

Without thinking she walked towards the teachers' quarters. She hesitated before going in but decided to do it anyway. What did she have to lose? Helen knocked on Peter's door but there was no answer. Feeling dejected, she turned around. She hadn't really expected for him to be there but felt disappointed all the same.

The rest of the day passed by. Helen simply went through the motions of reading her notes, having dinner and showering, and only when she was in bed did she allow the sadness that engulfed her to rip the cover. And she cried herself to sleep.

Monday morning went by fast. Helen was glad for the distraction of the lab test. It was a breeze, and she managed to keep her mind on the dissection. At 4:30 p.m. sharp Helen was at the doctor's office with Padma. The doctor confirmed what she already knew. She was almost eight weeks pregnant.

Helen had lied when the doctor asked where the father was. "He's in the army, posted in Jaffna."

The doctor gave her a sympathetic look, loads of information on prenatal care and a referral to an OB-GYN. At the end, she had told Helen to call her if she needed to talk. "Being pregnant can put a lot of pressure on you. I just want you to know that there is help, that is, if you want to reach out."

Helen simply nodded and left.

The rest of the week flew by. Helen went back to Peter's room every evening but couldn't catch him. But she knew he was there since one of the other lectures she ran into told her so. He had given her a quizzical look, and she felt embarrassed. Finally on Thursday as she was putting her equipment away after the chemistry lab test, she saw Peter through the lab window and was flooded with relief. But by the time she reached the corner where he stood with a group of students, he was gone. Out of breath and frustrated, Helen turned around and went back to her hostel. She was surprised to see Peter standing there momentarily forgetting what he had put her through. Relief spread through her mind as she greeted him with a big smile. "Peter, I was looking for you."

"I didn't want to bother you during exams, Helen, but today was the last, right?" It was partially true. He knew what he had to tell Helen probably wasn't what she wanted to hear. So, he decided to wait until her exams were over. As much as he would rather avoid this whole thing, he knew he couldn't. And time was not in their favor. "Helen, let's go somewhere private; can you meet me near the station in half an hour? We need to talk."

"Yes." Helen nodded, a glimmer of hope lifting her spirit up a little. Peter was waiting for Helen when she got to the station.

Peter took Helen to the Galle face hotel restaurant for tea.

"You should have told me we are coming here. I

would have dressed better," Helen chastised Peter happily. She felt lighthearted and happy even though she noticed how Peter walked ahead of her when she tried to hold his hand. She didn't want to dwell on it, not now. He asked her about her exams and if she wants to study further or remain a schoolteacher. Then they talked about where she might get her first appointment. Helen noticed how he talked about her future but stayed within the limits of her career. But she allowed him to steer the conversation and settled in to simply enjoying the pleasant afternoon. It was close to five when they finished tea and sandwiches and ribbon cake. For once Helen didn't feel nauseated at the sight of food. She happily gazed into Peter's eyes, devouring every word he said. He suggested they go for a walk along the beach. The sun would be setting in soon. They didn't talk much on the walk until they reached somewhat of a quiet spot on the beach and sat down on the pier.

The setting sun on the horizon casted a warm orange glow. It would be another hour and a bit before it disappeared, taking its light with it. The sound of the rolling waves, the noise of the people talking, laughing, buses and cars honking in the distance and constant cawing of the crows all came together in a chaotic symphony. Helen sat on the pier taking it all in, bathed in images and sounds of a world in constant motion, a world that wouldn't stop no matter what. A sense of melancholy washed over her.

Peter sat next to Helen watching her. There was so much sadness in her face. The carefree spirited eyes which challenged him in class were now filled with pain. Guilt washed over him, landing a gut punch. He closed his eyes with a sigh. He needed to get this done and over with. There was no point in dragging on what was inevitable.

"Helen, I went to see my friend, the doctor I mentioned the other day." Peter waited for Helen's reaction, but she sat there staring silently at the ocean. "There is a tablet he gave me, a pill for you to take. It is safe but you should take it before ten weeks, that's what's recommended."

Helen still didn't respond, but her body was shaking in silent sobs. Peter wanted to put his arms around her and console her, but he didn't dare. "Helen, please... I know this is painful. I know I sound heartless, but this is the best solution. Please, Helen, you need to understand, we cannot make an emotional decision here. We need to be smart. You need to abort the pregnancy."

Helen couldn't believe what she was hearing. Did she mean nothing to him?

"Best for you, you mean, because it certainly isn't the best solution for me or the baby." Helen shook her head. "No, Peter, getting an abortion is not the best solution for all of us."

"So what do you propose, Helen, that you keep this and raise it alone? Huh? How are you going to do that with a teaching job in some rural school all by yourself? What about your family, your parents, have you thought about the impact this decision will have on them? Helen, do the right thing." Peter was getting frustrated; he felt his heart palpitating. Shit, he had forgotten to take his blood pressure tablets in the morning.

"Right thing? The right thing, Peter, is for you to marry me. Not to ask me to get an abortion," hissed Helen through clenched teeth. How dare he preach about doing the right thing. "What you're asking me to do, it's risky and it is a sin, Peter. You are asking me to kill a baby."

"It's not a baby yet, Helen." Peter hated hearing the word baby. He had refused to see it that way. It was easier to suggest the abortion as long as he denied the existence of a baby, a fully formed life.

Helen shook her head "No, Peter, you want me to get rid of this so you can live your life like nothing happened. But my life will never be the same, ever again." How could he force her to do this? "Peter all this time, all the flirting, you can't tell me that I imagined everything. Did you not love me at all? Please, Peter, you are asking me to do this horrible thing, but you won't even consider marrying me?" Helen pleaded through tears.

"You are a very attractive girl, Helen, and no, you didn't imagine it. I was attracted to you," said Peter softly. He hadn't planned on admitting it, but he couldn't let Helen go on thinking that she didn't matter at all. She didn't deserve that. Seeing her broken like this made him feel sick to his stomach. But he also knew that attraction wasn't love.

"I can't marry you, because…" he hesitated but decided to come clean. "I'm engaged to another girl, Helen. I'm sorry."

There it was: the truth. Helen felt a fresh wave of sadness surge through her body escaping in a sob. She took a deep breath, looked at Peter and asked "Do you love her ?"

Peter nodded. "Yes, I have loved her all my life."

The sun had now almost set. It was being devoured by the ocean faster and faster. Within seconds the sun fully disappeared, taking its light and the warmth along with it. The street lights lit up in a feeble attempt to save the world from otherwise ubiquitous darkness. Peter and Helen sat there just staring into nothingness, each engulfed in their own sadness.

It was around 7:30 p.m. when Peter finally stood up and pulled Helen to her feet. It was dark and almost empty, other than a few people still walking along the pier. There was a drunk somewhere in the distance shouting something incoherently. Peter hailed a taxi and they both sat in silence until they got to the residence. Helen started walking towards her hostel without a word to Peter. She was feeling numb. Peter paid for the taxi and ran to catch up with her, but Helen didn't care. She had nothing to say. She felt strangely empty. Finally, when she reached the entrance to her hostel, Peter took her hand and covered her palm with his. This gesture startled her, and for a fleeting second, she felt a hope she didn't know that still existed in her. He turned around and left, and she opened her palm to see a small case with a tablet.

CHAPTER 15
End of a Journey

Saturday morning, all the bags were packed, and the hostel room Padma and Helen shared for three years was completely empty, apart from the beds and the table and chairs. An end of a journey with so many memories made along the way. They came here as young, naïve girls out of the protective arms of their parents for the first time in life. Now after three years they were leaving this place they called home to embark on another journey as adults. It was bittersweet.

Helen was dreading it. She had spent a couple of agonizing days staring at the tablet Peter had given her. Padma had tried to encourage her to take it, to go through the abortion before going home. But Helen couldn't. In the end, she threw the tablet in the garbage. She was scared and anxious. She didn't know how to tell her parents or what her next step was. But through the fears and sadness, two things had become clear to her. She was not going to get an abortion and Peter was going to marry her.

The next few weeks felt like an eternity for Helen. What should have been a happy homecoming was torture. Her parents and her brother and sisters were elated to have her home. She was the first to have flown the nest on her own to study, and now she would be going away again on her own to start her job. She looked at the excited faces of her younger siblings, looking up to her in awe, and she felt ashamed. They all came to her graduation ceremony and looked on, brimming with pride.

Helen saw Peter sitting on the stage with other lecturers looking distinguished, and her heart ached. Her friends looked at him loathingly. Sarath and Nimal refused to shake hands with him. Helen had told her friends about the pregnancy a few days before the ceremony. They were furious with Peter. Sarath, who had secretly carried a torch for Helen, had vowed to make Peter do the right thing. They were going to speak to Peter and force him to marry her. It was the right thing to do. Her father boasted to his friends about how proud he was of his eldest daughter, of her achievements. Her mother, her sweet, innocent mother, made all her favourite dishes. She was proud of her daughter yet wasn't quite sure how she felt about a young, unmarried girl going away from home on her own to work. But her husband said it was something to be proud of, and she saw other girls Helen's age doing the same, so she believed it was the case. This was a new generation, different from their day, she told her neighbourhood ladies who gathered around the gate in the afternoons.

Helen watched and listened and smiled, trying hard to mask the guilt she felt. She knew in a few weeks' time all of this happiness would turn to dust and her parents would be destroyed. She would be the talk of the town, the downfall of this proud man, her father, a pillar in the community, a respected leader. She felt the pain her mother was going to feel, the look of awe in her siblings' eyes turned to disappointment. It was unbearable. Finally, her letter of appointment arrived, and Helen was relieved. At last, she didn't have to continue with the charade. She wouldn't be able to keep her pregnancy a secret much longer. Her clothes were getting tighter, and her body was changing.

On December 28, Helen hugged her mother, her sisters and her brother and said goodbye as she left with her father to take the train to Matara. Her first teaching appointment was at a school in a small town about 15 km from the coastal town of Matara. Her father arranged for her to stay with a family he knew. Helen had already arranged to change accommodations soon after. She couldn't stay with her father's friends and hide the pregnancy. So Sarath had come through for her and found a nice family closer to her school who were willing to rent out a room.

Helen looked back at her family as the taxi pulled away and felt a wave of sadness wash over her. It felt like a final goodbye. In a way it was. She had let everyone down, bringing shame on her family. None of them would ever be the same. She closed her eyes and wept silently. Two weeks later she moved into the new place. It was a small house owned by an elderly couple. They lived by themselves. The elderly man was a retired postman, and they had one daughter who was married and lived in a different town. The woman reminded Helen of her own mother, a faithful wife and a doting parent. They both loved having Helen live with them. She reminded them of their daughter, they told her.

Helen's parents weren't happy about her move. Their unmarried daughter living with strangers was unsettling, and her father had visited her as soon as she told them. He was less concerned once he became acquainted with the family and was satisfied that his precious daughter, his first born, was in safe hands. Helen clinched with guilt. This was now going to be harder. Sarath had told the couple that Helen was married, and her father had now exposed her lie. The elderly couple sensed her discomfort but didn't say anything to correct her father. Helen was relieved. After her father left, she told the couple that she married one of her lecturers and hadn't told her parents yet because he was much older than her and a Christian. Well, it was partially true, thought Helen, trying to ease her guilt. Lately all she had done was to lie to everyone who cared about her.

Saturday January 27, 1973 Peter was onboard the train from Galle to Colombo with Velu. Peter was fighting hard to keep tears from falling. He felt helpless and it frustrated him. What was he going to do? How was he going to tell Anoma?" He had just gotten married to Helen the day before. He had tried everything he could to avoid it, but in the end he ran out of options.

Sarath and Nimal had come to see Peter after the graduation ceremony. Both the boys were angry and had called him a bastard. "You took advantage of an innocent young girl and now you're running away like a coward. Be a man,"Nimal had berated him.

Sarath, usually a mild-mannered young man, hadn't said much. But when Peter tried to explain that getting married for the sake of a baby was a life sentence for everyone, Sarath had spat in his face:"So you get on with your life and leave Helen with a life sentence?"

Peter had tried to reason that getting an abortion was still on the table as long as it was done right away. Sarath walked over to him threateningly, clenching his fist prompting Nimal to spring to his feet and hold his friend back.

"You asshole, the only way this is going to end is by you marrying Helen." shouted Sarath. Sarath was not a big man, but at that moment Peter had cowered before him, not out of fear but the guilt and embarrassment that emasculated him. The boys had threatened to go to the school board, and he knew they meant every word.

In the end, Peter ran out of excuses. He had gotten on a bus to see Velu, his dear friend, who implored him to marry Helen. He had no one on his side. The worst part was that Peter agreed with all of them. And he would have done it if it weren't for Anoma. He would take the responsibility and suffer the consequences if it didn't mean losing Anoma.

Then Anoma had flown in for Christmas for two weeks. He had begged Nimal to give him time until January and promised that he would marry Helen. Nimal had threatened to come see Anoma and tell her everything. Peter pleaded for more time, and Nimal had let it go at that.

They knew that Helen had a crush on Peter; they

had witnessed her flirting abashedly with him at times. Something which irritated some of the other girls. Sarath had once told her she was playing with fire. But Helen just laughed it away and denied having any feelings for Peter. The man was not who they thought he was, anyway.

Peter had not been able to pick up Anoma from the airport when she arrived. Part of him was glad that he couldn't. He wasn't ready to tell her anything about what was going on with him and he didn't want to lie either. He was glad that Christmas was always a time buzzling with family and friends as it kept both him and Anoma busy. She knew something was wrong with him and kept pestering him about it. Fortunately, they never found themselves alone long enough for her to crack his shield. Frankly he didn't think he would be able to keep this secret from her. It was eating away at him. But he didn't know what to tell her.

Something that Melvin had said to him had been turning the wheels in his head. Melvin told him about a couple, distant relatives of his, who were childless and had been looking to adopt a baby. They were wealthy, educated and good people. If Helen was willing, *only* if she was willing, he would talk to them. As crazy as it sounded Peter has been entertaining the idea in his mind. Maybe he could convince Helen to give up the baby, and once the baby was out of the picture, Helen would give him a divorce.

Velu had laughed at the idea. As much as Peter knew how crazy it sounded, he was desperate. He was willing to try anything to save his relationship with Anoma. In the end, he couldn't get himself to come clean to her. When he dropped her off at the airport, he hugged her and cried. Anoma knew then that something was wrong, but all Peter said was that everything will be fine.

"Trust me, just this once. Please?"

She nodded as she left but couldn't shake this feeling that everything was far from ok.

CHAPTER 16
No More Aces to Play

When Helen walked into the registrar's office in Galle, donned in a white saree. She looked nothing like a bride. Rather, like a young woman clad in white mourning the death of someone she loved. Nimal and Padma had come to pick her up from her place early in the morning. Helen lied to the elderly couple who had become like a mother and a father to her, saying she was going to a funeral. In a way she wasn't really lying. She didn't feel like a young bride getting ready to marry the love of her life. There was no sense of excitement of walking into a happy blissful wedded life. Instead, there was this feeling of doom looming over her head. There was a sense of undeniable grief knowing that her dream of a beautiful wedding, stepping on to the adorned poruwa, the wedding podium, dressed in a white lace saree to the sounds of ceremonial drums, were all part of a dream that would never be fulfilled. So, in a way she was going to a funeral. She was burying all her dreams that had died.

Peter and Helen got married on Friday January 26, 1973 at 2:15p.m. Afterwards, Peter offered to take Helen back to her place. It was awkward, but he had no intention of sharing a bedroom with Helen. He saw the shock register on Nimal's face, but surprisingly Helen looked relieved. Helen no longer held on to any hopes of romance with Peter. Love, trust sounded like empty words to her. And this marriage to her was a mere necessity. It was necessary for her survival, to protect her and her family from shame and embarrassment. Everyone would get over that she had eloped, but none of them would have been able to escape the shame it would bring her family should the world find out that she gave birth to a child out of wedlock. The last thing Helen wanted was to be alone with this man who had crushed all her dreams.

"Yes Peter you don't have to stay with me on our wedding night," laughed Helen sarcastically. "But you will come to drop me off at home so I can introduce you to Aunty Prema and Uncle George." She was firm on that. The older couple had been wondering when they would get to meet Helen's husband. Prema was already suspecting that a husband wasn't the only thing Helen was hiding. Prema was a woman and a mother. She might be naïve and lacking knowledge of the world outside, but she recognized a pregnant woman when she saw one.

It was late when they arrived at Helen's place. Peter flinched when Helen introduced him as her husband. Despite the old couple insisting they stay for dinner, Peter stated that they needed to catch an early train back to Colombo from Galle.

Nimal hadn't said anything to Peter on the drive back. He didn't try to mask his dislike of Peter either. Velu made small talk trying to break the awkwardness while Peter sat in the back, feeling defeated and like he couldn't care less about making conversation. He couldn't relate to the person he had become. His sense of pride, self-respect, all gone. He was now nothing more than a coward living a lie. Married to a woman he does not love, lying to the woman he loves, leading a double life ridden with guilt. Peter closed his eyes and tilted his head back as a solemn tear trickled down from the corner of his eye and disappeared into the sideburns.

"You did the right thing. Leave your past in the past, Peter, and make it work," Velu said with a pat on Peter's back as they walked back to the hotel room that night. Peter nodded and went to his bed. He wanted to scream, cry, and punch something. He still hadn't told Anoma. Even if he convinced Helen to give up the child for adoption, she might not agree to a divorce. And how on Earth was he going to convince Anoma to agree with this plan? It sounded ridiculous, even in his mind. The odds were stacked against him. Any fool could clearly see that. But he must try. He wasn't a gambler. In fact, gambling and alcohol were two things he never touched, thanks to his father who abused both. Yet here he was, gambling all while holding no aces.

"I brought you a cup of tea," Aunty Prema came into her room without invitation, an annoying habit that irritated Helen.

"Thank you," muttered Helen as Prema put the cup down and sat down at the end of the bed. Helen was in her nightdress, and it showed her growing belly. She pulled the covers over her, conscious of Prema's intrusive glance. The old woman was kind and caring but also curious with little respect for others' privacy.

"About four months now?" Prema was direct, another annoying thing about the sweet old woman.

"Yes," nodded Helen. There was no point in lying anymore. Her belly was growing, and she was married, the last hurdle.

For the first time Helen didn't feel ashamed in admitting that she was pregnant. In fact, she felt strangely relieved. Until Peter signed the papers,

Helen grappled with the fear of facing the world pregnant and alone. What this marriage meant was yet to be discovered, but at least she was married.

"Due in June," said Helen, forcing a smile.

"Your mother must be excited. Let me tell you, child, being a grandmother is like being given a second chance in life…" Prema continued with her monologue about her grandchildren. Helen nodded occasionally, pretending to listen, but her mind was occupied with something else. She must tell her parents soon. She was expected to be home in April for Sinhala and Tamil new year, and she would be seven months pregnant. Now that she was married to Peter, at least it wouldn't be a complete disaster. But still she knew there would be questions and accusations. This was not going to be as happy a homecoming for her as it would if she had her parents' blessing and was going home to deliver the news of their first grandchild. She had eloped with a man her parents would never approve of and now she was pregnant. Her father was not a fool, and if Prema had proven anything, it was that her sweet, old-fashioned mother wouldn't be fooled either. Helen could take her father's anger, but she couldn't face his disappointment.

"I thought he would stay tonight. Helen…?" Aunty Prema was still babbling.

"Sorry, Aunty,I am just tired. Peter had to go back home. His mother isn't feeling well,." said Helen, putting her teacup on the bedside table.

Taking the cue, Aunty Prema got to her feet and picked up the empty cup. "If you need anything just let me know. You need to take care of yourself and the baby now. No more long trips," said the older woman as she left, closing the door behind her.

Helen sunk into her pillow and closed her eyes. She must talk to her parents soon. The old couple knew, and the last thing she wanted was for her father to find out from them. But what was she going to tell them?"Congratulations, Mom and Dad, you are going to be grandparents. By the way, I am married, and my husband is 20 years older than me and in love with another woman."

The Other woman. Helen's mind wandered in a direction she had tried not to go. The deathly pallor of Peter's face as he stood up after signing the marriage form had pierced through Helen's heart like a sharp knife. It had taken all she had not to break down in tears in front of the marriage official. Peter obviously loved this woman very much. Helen felt a desire to know about this woman; what was she like? Was she pretty? Was she educated? She remembered how Peter often commented on her lack of knowledge on current world affairs and wondered if this other woman was more sophisticated. Helen felt a pang of jealousy sear through her. Well, he was her husband now. Helen felt hatred towards this woman she had never met. And without any warning, a wave of self-pity washed over her, and she let the tears roll down freely.

CHAPTER 17
Web of Lies

As the next few weeks passed by, Helen fell into a mundane cycle of work, home, doctors' appointments and hiding herself in her room apart from meals in order to avoid explaining to the old couple why her husband wasn't visiting her. She had run out of excuses. So, every Friday evening she lied to the old couple, pretending to go home with Peter and instead visiting Padma over the weekend.

Helen had continued to call Peter and tell him about the pregnancy after each doctor's visit. Conversations were very short, curt, and she could feel how uncomfortable he was every time she mentioned the baby. And every time she asked when he was going to visit her, he made excuses. Even though he didn't say anything, she knew he was irritated with her for pressuring him to visit. As much as Helen tried to be strong, she knew she was fighting a battle that was already lost. It left her depressed.

One evening, on a Saturday when she was visiting Padma, they went to the beach. As Helen sat there staring into the sunset, listening to the sound of crashing waves, she pictured herself walking into the ocean. What if she ended her life? All the pain, the shame, would be gone. But what then? When they discovered the body, they would know she was pregnant. It would be in papers. It would bring shame to her family regardless. There was no way out. Helen couldn't stop herself from crying and her whole body was shaking with sobs. Padma put her arms around her friend and the two of them stayed at the beach until Helen calmed down.

She told Padma how she was feeling suicidal at times. "Don't worry, I won't do it. It was just a thought." With a weak smile, Helen tried to reassure her friend, who looked worried.

That week after Helen went back, Padma took matters into her own hands. She wrote a letter to Peter threatening to expose what an asshole he was if he doesn't get his act together. She urged him to accept the fact that he was now married to Helen and to act like it. If Helen died by suicide, her blood would be on his hands.

Peter had panicked at the thought of Helen's suicide. He was angry at her and himself for the predicament they were in, but he didn't want her to be harmed. Peter still hadn't told Anoma about his marriage to Helen, and lying had become somewhat easy with time. As long as he didn't see Helen, he could tolerate the weekly phone calls and go on pretending to be single. He kept postponing the inevitable truth. But the thought of Helen taking her life finally forced him to accept that his life had changed. He could not go on being in denial.

He wrote to Anoma, explaining everything. He had begged her not to give up on him, on them. He told her about the couple willing to adopt the baby and assured her of a divorce once the baby was born. He of course didn't mention that none of this had been discussed with Helen.

That Friday, he got on the train. He stayed in Galle on Friday and told Helen that he would visit her on Saturday. She was disappointed but happy to see him nonetheless. They went for a walk after lunch, and he told her about the letter he received from Padma.

"I don't want anything to happen to you, Helen. I care about you. Everything was happening so fast, and I wasn't ready for this. I'm sorry you are going through this; believe me, I didn't mean to hurt you."

He hadn't said he loved her. But he said he cared about her, and Helen held on to that. "I wasn't ready for any of this either, Peter. This is not how I anticipated my life to work out. But we don't have a choice now." She wanted to say "I love you" but she didn't. It hurt too much to say that and not have it reciprocated.

When it was time for Peter to leave, Helen hugged him. She felt him stiffen. Then he gently tapped her on the back before pulling away. Helen felt a glimmer of hope. Like a little girl with a piece of candy, she savored that moment, a visit from her husband. "People learn to love each other once they get married." Helen's mother's words rang in her mind. For the first time in weeks, she went to sleep without crying.

Next weekend Peter came to visit her again on Sunday with Velu. They were both visiting a friend from their days in university over the weekend. Why didn't you take your wife to visit your friend? Or you could have stayed here "Said Prema aunty good naturedly. "Oh it was a lot of drinking with the men, you know..not the place for a pregnant woman" Peter had lied easily. Helen was irritated but she didn't want to complain, especially in front of others.

That Thursday, Peter received a call from Anoma. When the operator asked if he wanted to accept the call, his heart started pounding so loud he was sure the operator could hear it. Anoma cried and then screamed at him. She asked if this was his way of getting revenge. Finally, before she hung up, he begged her to come back so they could talk this through. She hadn't said yes, but she didn't break up with him either. That was a good sign. Peter sighed with relief.

The next weekend when Peter went to visit Helen, he asked Padma if Helen could stay with her. He wanted to speak to Helen about the adoption but didn't want to do it at Helen's place in case she made a scene. Peter didn't want the old couple to hear them. There was nothing in this plan of his that made him proud. As embarrassed as he was of his agenda, he wasn't ready to give up on the life he planned with Anoma either. Of course, Helen, who had no inkling about what Peter was going to suggest, was elated when he showed up to pick her up for a weekend away. She happily told Aunty Prema that she and her husband were going away for the weekend.

The drive to Galle was uneventful. Helen chatted happily and told Peter about the next doctor's visit. Asked him if he would like to come but he made an excuse saying he can't take leave from school. Peter mostly drove in silence with an occasional short response to a question from Helen.

They had an early dinner at a restaurant near the

beach and afterwards went for a walk. On the way back Peter pulled the car over to watch the sunset. They brought a couple of drinks and sat by the car on the beach. Helen decided to ask Peter about introducing him to her parents. Sinhala and Tamil new year was just a few weeks away and she needed to tell them before she went home for the holidays. She planned on writing a letter that week. She wanted Peter to come with her, that is, if her father didn't completely disown her and ban her from visiting. She also thought it was time that Peter introduced her to his family. She knew that his father had died long ago, but that's all she knew.

"Helen, how do you think your parents will react when they find out that you're married and seven months pregnant already?" Peter chose his word carefully. Helen sighed but didn't say anything. Her eyes filled up with tears. She knew exactly what they would say. She just hoped that if Peter was there, it would somehow be easier.

"It will destroy them," said Helen, wiping a tear. "I know what they will say and how they will feel. There's nothing I can do to change it… so why are you asking me this?" What was he getting at, seriously? Helen was beginning to feel irritated.

Peter set his drink down on the hood of the car with a sigh and walked towards the shoreline. He turned around and looked at Helen who was staring at him with squinted eyes.

"Helen, my father died when I was very young. He was not a very nice man. He gambled and drank. All I remember of him was coming home pissed drunk and screaming at my mother, asking for money to gamble, and my mother crying softly into the night, trying to hide the tears and bruising from us. I was too small to do anything, but I remember wishing that he was dead. And finally, when he died, do you know what I felt? Nothing. Not even a sense of relief. I felt nothing. But my mom cried." Peter let out a dry chuckle and continued. "My grandmother often pleaded with my mother to leave the bastard, come home with the children. But she didn't. I never asked her why, but I suspect that it wasn't just the religion, and all this marriage is for better or for worse bullshit. I think that despite all the misery, she loved my dad or at least the idea of a husband. She was a prisoner of her own beliefs and principals."

Helen shifted on her feet uncomfortably at those words. "Once you start loving someone it doesn't just go away," she said in almost a whisper.

"Right." Peter laughed and shook his head, irritating Helen even more.

"Anyway...Helen, I'm telling you this story so

that you understand. So that you know you have the power to control your future despite the mistakes we make."

Helen was getting uneasy, but she didn't say anything and let Peter continue.

"I have three brothers and a sister, Helen. With everything they have witnessed, you would think that my brothers would think twice before touching a drink, right? But no, they followed the same path. Sure, they weren't as bad as my father. At least they didn't gamble, but they like their alcohol as much as our father did. Each of them with six or seven kids, a single income and half of it spent on alcohol, the lives of their wives aren't all that different from my mother. Helen, I am the only son my mother has who doesn't drink or gamble. I am the only son who hasn't done anything to break her heart. With large families, I am who they rely on as well."

"My parents have high hopes for me too, Peter. They didn't exactly imagine their daughter dragging their names through mud," said Helen defensively.

"Exactly my point, Helen." Peter walked back to Helen and took her hand in his. "Your parents, my mother, they made sacrifices to get us to where we are now. We did this to ourselves, so it is our cross to bear. But our parents, my mother; she has been through enough."

Helen pulled her hand and instinctively put her hands around her belly. She wasn't sure what Peter was angling, but she had an uneasy knot in the bottom of her stomach. "I know all this; you don't think I have thought about it every single day for the past six months? But we can't hide this anymore. This baby is coming in three months…"

She saw Peter flinch and there were tears in his eyes. It softened her anger a little bit. He was feeling anxious. She knew that. "Peter, we will tell our parents together. They will be heartbroken, angry, but it will give them time to accept the reality. Once this baby is born, they will forget the hurt and the pain. It is their grandchild. They will love it. You know how babies bring families together." Helen truly hoped that it would.

"It's nice that you can be so optimistic." Peter shook his head. "It's not just the baby, Helen. What about you and me? What do you think will happen to your reputation? Do you think people in your town will forget about the scandal? You have sisters, don't you?"

Helen nodded her head. She wasn't sure where Peter was heading with this, but she had an uneasy feeling that he was teeing it up for something she wouldn't like. He had that same "I'm looking after your best interest" tone he had used on her before he tried to convince her to get an abortion. As well as the time he suggested reconstruction surgery.

"Helen, you know very well that this scandal will have an impact on their futures as well. Their future marital prospects will be that much harder." There wa a certain truth to what Peter was saying, and Helen knew that.

"The world doesn't need to know the baby was conceived out of wedlock. Peter, we are married, and we will tell them that we got married last year. It's not like we have to show our marriage certificate to the world," Helen argued back, trying to reverse whatever it was that Peter had in mind.

Peter felt slightly irritated. "You are naively optimistic, Helen, and you are only thinking about yourself and what is best for you."

"Huh? what is best for me?" How dare he accuse her of being selfish. Helen's temper was rising. "This baby is going to be born in three months. We cannot change that. What I am trying to do is to avoid a scandal, to save the reputation of our families. Sure, there will be talk, but we are married and that is that. And yes, our parents will be hurt, but it is too late to do anything about it now."

"Helen, I cannot tell my family this. I was engaged to another woman. We were getting married in August. For God's sake, the wedding invitations were supposed to go out in a few weeks." Peter choked at those words as Helen took a sharp breath. She was hurt. She was painfully aware of Peter's love for this other woman, and she didn't need reminders of that.

"How do I explain that I have a pregnant wife to my mother who is making plans for my wedding?"

Helen couldn't take it anymore. "I know you love another woman Peter, I know the last thing you want is to raise a family with me. But we are married, and you are going to be a father. So if you haven't told your precious girlfriend already, you should now."

"Helen, my friend, the doctor I told you about, he knows this couple. A wealthy couple who can't have children. They want to adopt the baby. They are good people. Educated, and they can provide a better life for the baby, a life free of stigma and all the baggage we have with us..."

Helen couldn't believe what she was hearing. Her head was spinning. She stared at Peter in disbelief. "You are a monster," screamed Helen. "You say that I am only thinking about myself, huh? First you wanted me to get an abortion and now you want to give our baby away to some strangers, so you can go home with your reputation intact? Pretend as if you are a saint?"She wished she had never met this man in front of her. "And then what? Once the baby is out of the way you're going to divorce me?"

Peter stood looking at her silently. He was conscious of people at the beach looking at them. The beach wasn't crowded, and it made them even more conspicuous. But he knew better than to try and calm Helen down. She was in shock and needed to get it out of her system. Peter had made up his mind. He didn't know if he and Anoma would have any future, but there would be no chance of it with a baby in the mix. What he had said about not being able to face his family wasn't a lie either.

Both Helen and Peter stood staring at the horizon where the sun was now rapidly disappearing. Hues of orange and red streaked the sky and the soft rolling waves alike. Soon it would give way to grays and almost black dark blues matching the melancholy of their spirits. Neither of them really noticed that it had gotten dark, nor that they were the only people at the beach, until the server at the restaurant came to collect their empty glasses.

Neither said a word to each other on the way back. Once they arrived at Padma's place, Helen got out of the car without so much as a goodbye to Peter. But Peter came around quickly and grabbed her hand.

"Helen, please. Please think about it. If there is ever a chance for us to be happy, you need to do this."

Helen kept staring at the ground. She couldn't look at him. "I wish I had never met you." Helen almost spat the words as she pulled her hand free and walked into the house without a backward glance.

CHAPTER 18
I Am Fighting for My Love

Padma knew something was wrong as soon as Helen walked in. At first, she couldn't believe that Peter had suggested giving the baby up for adoption. It felt so wrong. She felt a fresh wave of hatred and anger towards Peter. But in the morning Padma had a different take on the matter. She still hated Peter but told Helen that she understood why Peter would rather give up the child for adoption than admitting to his family his infidelity.

The society they lived in seldom forgave mistakes. Most people, especially women, only had two choices: bury their mistakes and lead a life of lies or pay the price. And the price was to be condemned to a life of shame. The degree may vary depending on one's status in society, but no woman escaped that. Divided by religion, race, caste, money, education and class, each person ticking any one of these boxes took pride in their status while looking down on those who they deemed lower.

Peter picked up Helen from Padma's house early on Sunday and drove her back to her place. Padma didn't even bother looking at Peter as she hugged her friend goodbye and completely ignored Peter when he said good morning. It cut through Peter like a knife. He remembered how Padma, along with other students, adored him. He loved being a teacher. He was good at it and took pride in knowing that his students not only respected him but loved him. He was fully aware of what Padma, Sarath and Nimal thought of him and probably others as well by now. The look of respect and adoration in their eyes was replaced with loathing. He was losing everything he had valued and loved in his life. It was the price he had to pay if he chose to fight for Anoma, the love of his life.

They drove in silence for the most part. Peter asked Helen if she was hungry, but she ignored him. She was starving, but she was angry and wanted him to know. She had contemplated taking the train back to her place, but that meant having to face Aunty Prema's interrogation. Helen was under no illusion that her world wasn't in shambles, but she was determined to glue it back together. And she was determined to show the world that she was in a happy marriage.

Peter pulled into a small roadside café for breakfast. Helen didn't argue, and Peter watched her wolf down string hoppers and dhal curry. She looked like a child. The sadness etched in her face and the anger in her eyes as of late were temporarily gone. Helen looked like her old carefree self. Peter sighed, trying to unburden himself from the guilt of knowing that it was him who destroyed that.

That week went by fast. Helen liked teaching, as she discovered. She was still fresh at her job, but it felt natural and she was at ease. The youth and whimsy of children soaking up knowledge made her forget her troubles. Sometimes she stayed after school to provide extra help. In no time she was the most popular teacher in that small village. Parents showed their appreciation by bringing small gifts, mostly food. She was popular with the staff as well. But she was wary of discussing details of her family, her husband or parents. She was vague whenever someone asked about her personal life and always changed the subject. At school she had created a haven where she could temporarily escape.

Peter hadn't come to visit Helen that weekend.

"I have to go home. I have to explain to my family that the wedding is off." Peter sounded irritated on the phone.

Helen was annoyed that he had waited this long

to call off the wedding. "We have been married for almost three months and you are just canceling your wedding? Were you hoping that you could somehow get married to your girlfriend in August?" As she said those words it dawned on her. "Oh my God, Peter, that's your plan. You want to give up the baby for adoption and divorce me so you can marry her!" Helen wanted to scream. Instead, she hung up the phone, went to her room and cried.

By the time weekend arrived, Helen finally came to the realization that Peter may never love her. She would probably end up alone, raising a baby on her own. Helen had tried hard to believe that Peter would come to love her. She was convinced that there was something between them, that he cared enough to have slept with her. She refused to believe that it was just sex. Once they got married, it gave her a small reassurance, a triumph in the sense that he now belonged with her, to her. Despite everything he continued to put her through she loved him deeply. And it broke her heart to realize that all he was thinking of was a way out.

As she lay in her bed that night, staring out the window at the dark sky strewn with millions of stars, Helen wondered about the couple Peter had mentioned. He had said that they were good people, wealthy, and that they could give a good life to her baby. Helen instinctively put her arms around her belly. She didn't want that train of thought to continue. She turned around and closed her eyes trying to block any thoughts of adoption. But they had already taken root in her mind and refused to stay buried. If Peter abandons her and the baby, how is she going to raise it by herself? She would have no money. She would be poor and alone with a baby. Helen felt a new fear take over her. She couldn't stop these thoughts; they kept swirling in and out of her mind even after she fell into a restless sleep.

By the time weekend arrived Helen knew she couldn't postpone writing to her parents much longer. Many times, she took a notebook and a pen to write a letter. But she didn't know how to even begin. At the end of the week, all she had written was "Dear Dad."

Peter received a letter from Anoma early that week saying that she didn't think their wedding in August was going to happen. She needed to decide about invitations and couldn't possibly go ahead with sending invitations out knowing full well that her fiancé was now a married man. Peter had immediately called Anoma begging her not to give up on them.

"Well, you let me know when you have the divorce, Peter," Anoma said before she hung up. He took the next bus home. He knew there would be panic and pandemonium with both families, his and Anoma's, trying to figure out the reason and who to blame.

Peter was sitting in the living room with his mother and sister. They were both crying. "How could she do this again? She destroyed us once. I should have never allowed her near you, us .." His mother cried in indignation, accusing Anoma of hurting him. Anoma has called off the wedding. She hadn't told them the reason but just that they are not getting married in August. Alice, of course, instantly concluded that Anoma had hurt her son again.

"It's not what you think. We are trying to figure things out. I am the one to be blamed for this." Peter tried to interject.

"What do you mean it's your fault? Is there another woman?" Alice looked alarmed.

But Peter couldn't bring himself to tell them the truth. He simply shook his head and said, "It's complicated. Just don't get into it with Anoma's parents. Please, Mom, it's not Anoma's fault."

That night, Peter felt breathless. The vein on the side of his forehead was throbbing furiously. He reached for his blood pressure tablets on the bedside table. He couldn't remember if had taken them today. He counted the remaining pills and it seemed like he had missed more than one day. Peter took a tablet with some water and lay back on the bed. "How long is he going to be able to keep this a secret? Up until now it was just Helen and Anoma he had to deal with. Now his mother and his family are involved too. Each passing day the noose is tightening around his neck. "Would it be easier if it snuffs him out of life? It would be, wouldn't it? No more Helen, no guilt, No more of enduring the loathing looks of his once beloved students gave him. None of that..You coward" Screamed his subconscious.

Finally, after tossing and turning in his bed for an hour or so, he got up and went to the kitchen where his mother was cooking dinner. Her eyes were red from crying. Peter felt a pang of guilt sear through him. He has caused so much pain to so many women, people he really loved. He put his arms around his mother and kissed the top of her head.

"I'm sorry I hurt you, Mom., I messed up. This isn't Anoma's fault. I swear. I just need time to fix this. Please, Mom, can you trust me?" Of course, Alice would. This was her little boy, the perfect one, her pride and joy. She hugged him tight and nodded.

CHAPTER 19
Uphill Battle

When Peter visited Helen next weekend, he was determined to talk to her about their future. There was no point in hiding the fact he wanted no part in her or the baby's life. He was going to make Helen see that being trapped in a loveless marriage was simply torture. Without the burden of a baby, Helen too would have a chance of happiness. But if she insists on staying married he was going to show her how unhappy it will be. In Peter's mind Helen would soon begin to loathe him and will agree to a divorce.

Little did he know that Helen was not a woman who could be easily manipulated. The naïve young girl he met was no more. The pain of falling in love with the wrong man, the twist of fate that brought her world crashing down, matured her into a tenacious woman fighting for her survival. Helen knew she was fighting an uphill battle, but she had no intention of losing. No matter how hard it got, how painful it was, she wasn't going to let Peter destroy her. She wasn't going to let another woman take her love and her future away from her.

Both of them were battling for their love and future and to fulfill a dream they once dreamt. Neither realized that they were simply pawns in a game of chess in which destiny already plotted all the moves.

Peter and Helen went to the town center for a walk in the afternoon. Helen was torn between anger and happiness in seeing him. She was still angry that Peter hadn't called off his wedding to Anoma once they were married. At the same time her heart leapt in joy when Peter came to see her. She wasn't sure if he would come. And she forgot all her anger the moment he walked in. For a moment she felt like a little girl with a piece of delicious candy. "Why does it hurt so much to be in love? I must have really hurt another woman in my previous life". Karma, the justification to everything when one fails to acknowledge or understand consequences of one's action.

There was a small shop with trinkets, and Peter walked in without saying anything to Helen. She stood outside, pretending to look at the window displays while stealing glances at Peter, trying to figure out what he was buying. He came out with a small package and Helen felt a mixture of curiosity and happiness like a little girl excitedly waiting for a gift. When they went back to Aunty Prema's house Peter didn't come in. He stood outside near the gate, and opened the small package, showing a beautiful amethyst pendant.

Helen reached out with a smile. "It's beautiful." Helen had tears in her eyes as she took it.

"It is, isn't it?" said Peter as he took it back. Helen was confused and taken aback as she looked at him questioningly.

"Helen, I'm not going to beat around the bush here. You know I am in love with Anoma. You and I, we don't have a future together."He could see her eyes were filled with tears but he couldn't stop now. He had to get it out. "I will be there for you until you give birth, then you give the baby to this couple I told you about. It is all arranged. We will get a divorce and neither of us ever have to see each other again. You will be free to live your life. You will find happiness, Helen. Both of us will." I'm sorry but I cannot commit to a life of misery when there is a solution"

Tears were streaming down Helen's face as she struggled to get words out of her mouth. But all she could do was stifle a sob.

"Anoma is coming next week, and I will be going

to see her," Peter said, holding up the pendant.

Those words pierced through Helen's heart like a knife. The pendant was for Anoma! How could he be so cruel? How could any human being be so vicious? Helen was seething with anger as the initial shock at Peter's cruelty wore off.

"You are a horrible, horrible man. You ruined my life, my future, my parents. You took everything from me. *I will never give you a divorce!"*

Helen screamed before turning around to see Aunty Prema standing at the doorway. She didn't care. She still couldn't believe how cruel Peter had been. The old woman looked at Helen with concern but didn't pry. She knew something really upsetting had happened. She long suspected that Helen was hiding something about her marriage. It broke her heart to see this promising young woman, a little younger than her own daughter, suffering like this. Prema didn't follow Helen into her room like she usually would have. Instead, she stood by Helen's closed bedroom door, listening to the sobs coming out. Prema then went and made a cup of tea, brought it to Helen and lightly caressed her head as she put it down beside the bed, whispering, "Life is hard my dear, but you are going to be a mother. You will learn to be tough. I will go to the temple and pray for you."

Helen couldn't sleep that night. She had cried for hours. Finally, around two in the morning she pulled herself up and started writing a letter to her parents. She poured her heart out, begging her parents to forgive her for what she had done, the shame she had brought on them, for disappointing them. Still, she didn't mention Peter wanting a divorce or being in love with someone else. That was not something she could admit to anyone. Only Padma, her best friend, knew the whole truth. Helen was hurting, broken into a million pieces. Yet amidst all this she knew one thing for certain: she will never let Peter go. She will figure out the baby, perhaps her parents will help convince Peter to keep the baby. But she will not give him a divorce. Her future, her survival, depended on their marriage. Building a life as a divorced woman was not something Helen could comprehend. There was no positive outcome to that, at least not in her mind.

Helen called in sick on Monday. She had stayed up all night, crying and pouring her heart out on the letter to her parents. She knew it would shock them and she was scared yet she felt a huge weight off her chest once she put the letter in the mailbox. Whatever came next, she knows her mother would not abandon her. She needed her family now more than ever. She felt a melancholic sadness settle in as she thought about her mother. Her sweet, naïve, uneducated mother. Helen had always regarded her mother as lackluster. Her mother was content being a dutiful wife and a doting mother and didn't aspire to be anything more. And Helen found this mildly irritating, a feeling which she hadn't cared to hide much. Now she felt a sense of guilt, remembering those moments.

When she arrived home from school one night, she saw a car parked outside. She didn't recognize it. But it didn't take her long to guess when she heard voices coming from inside. She froze when she heard the familiar, deep voice of a man and her heart started beating fast. She took a deep breath and slowly entered the house.

"We gave her everything she needed, she wanted the freedom to go away, and I trusted her. She was a stubborn child, always," her father was saying as he paced up and down the hallway.

Her mother was softly crying. Helen stood there at the doorway, looking at them, guilt, shame, helplessness all engulfing her, unable to utter a word, until Aunty Prema saw her. Then her mother came to her almost in a run. The anger and disappointment were all gone, replaced with relief of seeing her precious child. Both of her parents had been upset beyond words when they read her letter.

The letter had arrived on Thursday. At first her father had been angry and had vowed to disown her, but as they read the letter, concerns for her wellbeing had grown. Helen had said she was married to this Peter fellow, but it didn't seem like she was happy. She had mentioned that she thought about suicide but didn't because that would bring shame to her family. Why would she want to take her life if she was happily married? It didn't sound like their daughter. Helen's mother had wanted to visit her right away, but her father had been just too angry. It has been nothing short of a funeral at home that night. Helen's mother and the sisters had cried all day while her brother furiously raved, swearing to avenge his sister's honor. By nightfall, her father's anger had faded, and his heart ached for his daughter.

Just a few months ago he proudly watched his daughter graduate.

"Teaching is a good career for a woman, my Helen, stubborn and smart." Helen's father chuckled. "Always had a mind of her own, she will become a headmistress," he boasted to his friends, beaming with pride. Helen had stubbornly refused to consider the marriage proposal he had brought up, which irked him at the time. When his friend talked to him about his son and how wonderful a union between their children would be, Helen's father was elated. He was planning to invite his friend and his son over for a meal over

Sinhala and Tamil new year celebration in a couple of weeks when Helen was home for school vacation. It would have been a nice introduction, and Helen's father was sure the boy would change Helen's mind. But now all those hopes and dreams disappeared into darkness. He felt a sudden rage towards this unknown man who had stolen his daughter's heart along with all their dreams.

"Oh, my sweet child, my Helen." That's all her mother said. For a while both Helen and her mother cried. Her father didn't say anything but watched his daughter and his wife pensively. Finally, he came over and sat next to them.

"Helen, this guy, he is a lecturer you said?" asked her father gently, but there was a certain firmness in his voice.

Helen nodded.

"Did he, did he pressure you into this, Helen?" His voice cracked slightly, betraying his distress.

Helen forced herself to look at him. "No, he didn't. And we are married," she reassured him before he could ask. "I'm sorry, Dad, I really am. Please forgive me. I didn't think you would ever approve of him." Helen was crying again.

But her father abruptly stood up at those words. "Stop, Helen, do you take me for a fool? Huh? You didn't elope because you thought I wouldn't approve of this man. You eloped because you got pregnant. You were always stubborn, you refused to listen to us and now…now look at you…You make it sound like you wanted this marriage. If he loves you, why did he make you write a letter to us instead of being by your side and meeting us?"

Helen didn't answer him or dare look at him. She didn't have the courage to lie to his face. She wanted to tell the truth, unburden herself. But she knew if she told them that Peter was in love with another woman, that he wanted to divorce her, it would ruin whatever chance she may have of ever building a life with Peter. She couldn't face it if her father lost all respect for Peter. Helen was determined to win that battle with Peter. And that's a battle she had to fight on her own. Her parents, her family, could never know the truth about how horrible Peter had treated her or that he was not the stand-up guy she painted him to be.

Helen's father shook his head. "You're hiding something Helen, there's more to this. At least now, listen to me, smarten up and tell me the truth." Her father pressed on. Finally, Helen relented and told them that she got pregnant before they got married and Peter didn't want his family to know.

"He says it will be a problem if his family finds out. That it will be a scandal. So he wants to give the baby up for adoption." She revealed half the truth through tears and told them about Peter's plan.

Helen's mother burst into tears at that. But her father remained silent. He sat down with his head bowed and sighed. "So, your husband knows a couple who wants to adopt the baby?" he asked cautiously.

Helen felt uneasy. She didn't like the tone in her father's voice. "I haven't met them, and I think we can raise the baby. Peter's family will eventually accept it" Helen was looking for reassurance from her parents. But neither of them said anything.

Helen's parents stayed with her that weekend. Her mother finally stopped crying by Saturday morning and despite the predicament they were in, Helen was thankful to have them by her side. Her mother fussed over her, and her father maintained an uncomfortable silence. He asked if Peter was coming that weekend; he wanted to meet him. Helen lied and said he had to go home as his mother was not feeling well. The truth was that she didn't think he would. She really didn't want to deal with what could go down when her father met Peter that weekend. Dealing with her parents and Peter's cruelty had been more than enough. Peter had said Anoma was visiting. Perhaps it was a lie. The more she thought about what he did (buying a gift and then asking her, his wife, if she thought it was nice before saying it was for another woman) was cruel. Helen was sure he did that to change her mind. He was probably hoping that she would agree to a divorce if he was mean to her.

Sunday morning, her parents left to go back home. It was a tearful goodbye. They thought it would be best if she didn't come home for the new year holidays.

"If your husband wants to give the baby away, it is best that no one finds out about it. You can't be seen like this. People talk, Helen, and you have your sisters to think about." Helen knew what her father was saying made sense, but it hurt her feelings all the same. She was shunned from society. Her marriage was not saving her from this shame. She felt angry at Peter, society, her fate, but there was nothing she could do. What future was she going to have as a divorcee?

Next few weeks just flew by. Peter came to visit her the weekend after her parents visited. Helen told him about what she told her parents and asked if his mother knows. When he told her that she doesn't Helen firmly said "Well Peter, I am never giving you the divorce you want. You have a choice; you can accept that we are married and give our marriage a chance, to be happy or you can choose to be miserable with me for the rest of your life"

CHAPTER 20
Do as Your Husband Says

By April new year holidays, Helen was seven months pregnant, and by the time school started again she would be close to eight months. Her parents wanted her close by for her last trimester. They had consulted an OB-GYN at the De Soysa Maternity hospital in Colombo and wanted her to move closer. Yet she could not be home with them as Peter and Helen had not come to an agreement on the adoption. Peter too agreed that it would be best if she moved to Colombo, which was closer to him as well. That meant he could visit her more often and help her with doctors' appointments which would become frequent. Peter managed to find a rental place, a room closer to the hospital, just before the holidays. Helen said goodbye to the old couple, Aunty Prema and Uncle George, who had become her family in this short time. Aunty Prema had tearfully asked Peter to take care of Helen, to change his mind about giving the baby up for adoption. Peter was annoyed that more people were in the know of his plans. Uncle George, a man of few words, had said, "A man is judged not by his mistakes but how he amends them." Peter didn't say anything.

Helen put in a request for vacation from school. She would soon be on maternity leave anyway. She looked at the school as they drove by. So many things had happened in the last few months. The only source of happiness during these dark days was that school. And now she was leaving that behind, too. She didn't know what was going to happen once her maternity leave was over. Was she going back to the same school? Where was Peter going to be? Helen had been trying not to think about the baby much. Her parents seemed to agree with Peter as well. Her father had said that if Peter wanted to give up the baby for adoption, Helen should do that. Her mother hadn't said anything, but her silence meant she too agreed with them. Even Padma, her best friend, had told her as much.

The room Peter had rented for Helen was in a small house near the hospital. The house was rather basic, a three-bedroom house with just one washroom shared by the dwellers. The owner was a middle-aged woman, a widow who lived by herself. She rented the room out to people like Helen, mostly women and sometimes small families that needed temporary accommodation for hospital visits. It was a far cry from the warmth and the love Helen experienced with . People who rent here were seldom happy. They carried the burden of pregnancies, like Helen, or sickness. The other room was currently empty. The landlady informed Helen and Peter that it was just vacated a couple of weeks ago by a young father who needed to visit his infant son and wife at the hospital daily. The infant was sick for months. "It gave me a steady income," the woman said with regret, not because the baby didn't make it, but because the end of the infant's life meant it was the end of her steady income. Helen suddenly found herself thinking of the little unfortunate baby who would never see what the world has to offer.

"This is all I could find. I will look for a better place," Peter whispered. He looked visibly shaken as well.

The first few days, Peter came to visit Helen every day. It was a welcoming change. They avoided any discussion about adoption or whether he told his family about her. Helen just wanted to enjoy the moment. It felt almost normal, as if Peter cared about her, and Helen was afraid of shattering that. Peter couldn't shake the depressing ambience of the house either. It haunted him even after he went back to his room in the college residence, Helen's face full of fear and helplessness kept coming back to him. It was different than when she told him she was pregnant or all the times he had hurt her in the past few months. Even though she was hurting, there was a glint of self-perseverance, strength behind her eyes. But it was different this time. She looked vulnerable, truly helpless like that fateful day when they were stopped by the army, almost eight months ago. So Peter, despite his resolution to convince Helen to leave him, couldn't bring himself to hurt her anymore.

Peter didn't bring up the subject of adoption either. He had spoken to the couple and had reassured them that they would get the baby. The couple was distantly related to Melvin, and Peter had gone to visit them at their home. The couple, Anura and Sriya De Silva, were quite wealthy, and they had a lovely home. The woman reminded him of his own mother in her demeanor. Both were educated, Anura a surveyor and Sriya a teacher. Peter felt certain that they would be good parents and the baby would have a good life with them. A life surrounded by love. A far better life than what he and Helen could give. The child would be free of the hurt, betrayals and hatred that surrounded its birth.

On Sunday April 14, 1973, it was Sinhala and Tamil new year day. Helen sat alone in her room looking at the plate of milk rice, lunumiris (chilli chutney), and a few sweets. She hadn't touched it and wasn't hungry either. She had been crying the whole day. Peter had gone home that weekend, and she had been all alone for a couple of days now. Her mother had come to visit her with her brother on Friday. She brought her rice, eggplant, her favourite, and all her other favourite food. Her mother had not been able to hold back her tears. She had insisted on feeding Helen and kept repeating stories of her childhood. Helen knew it was her coping mechanism. When they left, her mother had promised to come back on Monday. Sunday was New year's day so she couldn't leave the house. Helen wanted to ask if her father was going to visit but dared not. She kept thinking of the celebration taking place at home. Her parents, her sisters, and her brother, all sitting at the table enjoying the festive meal together. And she was all alone, holed up in this miserable room all by herself.

Helen felt a fresh bout of tears stream down her face. Just then there was a knock at her door. Helen wiped her face and opened the door to see her brother standing at the doorway with a bag full of food.

"Mom wanted me to bring you these," he said as he put down the food on the small table.

Helen burst into tears. "Tell mom I'm sorry," she sobbed. Her brother hugged her tight, wishing that none of this had happened.

"We are there for you, akka. You will never be alone".

Helen's mother came to visit her on Monday and spent the whole morning with her. She again brought a whole load of food. The woman who owns the house was happy with all the extra food and her demeanor towards Helen changed a bit. "I have seen girls like you, from good families, trusting the wrong man. Ruined their lives. Such a shame. "The woman said to Helen after her mother left. Peter came on Tuesday evening and promised to come every weekday after work. He kept his word.

Over the next few weeks, Peter or her mother accompanied her to the doctors' visits. Peter and her mother still hadn't met each other. Her mother would ask her if he came to visit but nothing more. She liked that Peter was visiting her every day and taking her to her appointments. She wondered if he had changed his mind about adoption. But then he would have told his family and she wouldn't need to be in hiding. She knew she had to talk to him. She had been thinking about the adoption and was beginning to understand what Padma and Peter had said about the scandal following all of them through their lives. Still, she couldn't help but wonder if Peter and she could stick together as a family so that they could weather it. They could be a family and not care about what anyone says.

In the end, Helen didn't have to broach the subject. Peter brought it up himself. They had another appointment, and the doctor said that the baby could arrive early. The due date was just two weeks away. Also, Anura and Sriya had wanted to meet Helen. Peter had mentioned that Helen had some reservations, and they thought if they could meet the mother, it would give Helen the assurance she needed. Peter didn't tell them that Helen was yet to agree to give up the baby. After Peter and Helen got back from the appointment, Peter decided to be direct with Helen.

"Helen, we need to talk about the adoption," he said.

Helen sighed and put her hand over her belly rubbing the spot where the baby had been kicking. Peter's eyes were drawn to Helen's hand covering her stomach, and he quickly looked away. It felt wrong, as if he had no right to look at the baby. This life inside Helen he was responsible for was pricking at his conscience.

"Why can't we raise the baby, Peter? Why are you so adamant to give up your baby?" Helen's voice was pleading but calm. It was a good sign. Peter relaxed a little.

"I have hurt a lot of people. It is going to take a

long time to heal those wounds. A child needs a loving mother and a father. Right now, we are not those parents. Can you honestly say that you can look at me and forget all the pain I have caused you?"

Helen shook her head. There was no point pretending anymore. Yes, she loved him, but if she could turn back time, she wouldn't want him anywhere near her. There was so much pain.

"Exactly, and I don't care what anyone says. I know for a fact that if parents are not happy, children will not be happy either. They will know that something is wrong and they grow up to be unhappy adults, with trust issues, anger issues... because that's all they knew."

Helen kept staring outside the window. There was truth to what Peter was saying. Also, she didn't know Peter's family at all. Perhaps he was so adamant about hiding this because his family was rather uptight and conservative. They may never forgive her for breaking up Peter's engagement. Maybe they approved of this other woman. After all, she was a Buddhist and Peter was a Christian. She knew that her father would never have approved under normal circumstances.

"So, your mother, your family, they will never accept the baby?" Helen wanted to know.

"I cannot tell them, Helen, I just cannot. There's no

way I can face them." Peter shook his head.

"So it's not so much about your family as much as it is about you not wanting to face the truth?" Helen was too sharp to miss the ambiguity in Peter's reply.

Peter ignored that and pulled a photograph out of his pocket. "This is Anura and Sriya De Silva," he said, handing the photograph to Helen. "The couple who wants to adopt the baby. Helen, Anura is a surveyor and Sriya is a teacher. They are good people. I went to check out their house. They are wealthy, educated. They will give this child a chance to grow up in a loving and healthy environment. The child will be loved."

Helen stared at the couple in the photograph. They looked happy. It was taken outdoors, probably at the Kandy Botanical gardens by the looks of it. They seemed like a couple deeply in love. The kind of love she dreamt of. She kept staring at the picture for a while, then nodded and said, "Can I meet them?"

"Of course, In fact, they asked the same, you know. They want to meet the mother." Peter was quick to respond and Helen could hear the relief in his voice.

The next day, both Helen's father and mother came to visit her. She was surprised to see her father. Her mother fussed about her as usual while her father talked to the woman. Helen heard him giving the woman some money and instructing her to call a taxi if Helen went into labour. Then he asked Helen where Peter was. She told him that Peter came to visit her every day after work and saw her father's jaws tighten, but he didn't say anything.

Abruptly, he asked about the adoption. "Have you and your husband decided about the adoption? You are still here, so I guess he's going to keep it a secret from his family?"

Helen was taken aback by his bluntness. But she knew that her father was no fool. She told them about the couple who wanted to adopt and showed them the picture. Her father wanted to know their address. Helen was sure that he was going to do his own investigation.

She looked at her parents and realized how wrong she had been about them. She had never thought of her mother as a strong woman, but rather a timid, uneducated woman who knew nothing of importance. And her father, a stoic, old-fashioned man with archaic values. Her mother had proven the strength in her unconditional love for her children was enough to withstand all the insults and grief society would bring. Her father, despite his convictions, had proven that his love for his daughter transcended social norms of all times. For the first time in her life, Helen realized how unfair she has been towards them.

CHAPTER 21
Gift of Life

Helen and Peter met with Anura and Sriya on Saturday, May 26. They met at Melvin's house as Helen was too uncomfortable to sit for a long time at a restaurant. Besides, she didn't want to meet them at a public place. Helen felt embarrassed at first. Sriya was much older than her and looked kind. She spoke with a certain understanding towards Helen. Helen watched the couple, how attentive Anura was towards Sriya and how they held hands. They told her that they had been married for 15 years, and the doctors told Sriya that she couldn't get pregnant. She looked sad when she said it, and Anura instinctively put his arms around her. How wonderful it seemed to be loved like that.

Sriya reached over and squeezed Helen's hand. "Listen, Helen, I can promise you, we promise you, that we will give this baby everything a child needs, a good home, a good education."

Helen nodded. It was everything she couldn't give.

Sriya felt Helen's pain, but she also felt a slight fear. What if she changes her mind? Sriya and Anura could see that it was Peter who was pushing for the adoption. Melvin had told them that the pregnancy was an accident and that Peter was not in love with her, but he remained a great guy. He didn't sound like a great guy to Anura.

At the end of the visit, Helen finally made up her mind. If someone else was going to raise her baby, this couple would be the best to do it. She knew they would provide the loving, stable home that she couldn't.

For the next few days Helen had someone visiting her every day. Her mother came most mornings. Peter came every evening after work and Sriya and Anura came to visit once more. Helen cried again and told Sriya that she wished things were different.

"You are an educated woman, Helen; you will figure things out. Time will heal everything, you will find your happiness and you will have other babies." Helen wished she could believe Sriya's words. But right now, all she knew was that Peter still didn't love her. She was sure that once the baby was given up, Peter would ask for a divorce. If Peter ended up leaving her, she couldn't raise a baby on her own. That fear was part of the reason she agreed to go ahead with the adoption. But she didn't say any of that to Sriya.

Sriya's heart ached for this young woman who was about to give her the best gift of her life. "Helen, you and Peter can visit the child if you like. At least you will know how the baby is growing up." Sriya instantly regretted saying that, but she and Anura had discussed it. They really felt sorry for Helen after their first visit but also knew that both Peter and Helen could be trusted not to jeopardize the child's future once the adoption was done. He had spoken to Peter and despite whatever was making him do this, he looked and sounded like a trustworthy person. He has asked around about Peter and everyone spoke very highly of him. Melvin too had spoken very highly of him. Anura was old enough to understand that life was not always fair, and that seemed to be the case with Peter and Helen.

On Thursday May 31st evening Helen was admitted to the hospital. Peter was visiting her, and she had started getting contractions. Peter took her to the hospital and Helen was admitted.

On June 1, 1973 at 4:15 a.m., Helen gave birth to a beautiful, healthy baby girl of 7lb, 06oz. Once the baby was cleaned and Helen was back in the ward, the nurse brought the baby back to Helen and asked if she wanted to feed her. Helen looked at the beautiful baby girl sleeping peacefully. She cradled her in her arms and kissed her forehead. At that moment, nothing else mattered. She knew she would fight the whole world if she must to keep this precious child safe. There was nothing she couldn't do, nothing she wouldn't do to protect her. Helen then realized that she didn't care what Peter's family thought. She and Peter and this little baby that is all that mattered. Helen hoped and prayed that Peter would change his mind once he saw this precious child. How could he not?

After a while the nurse came to take the baby back to the nursery. But Helen didn't want to let go.

"Ok, a few more minutes. But you need your rest too. I will be back in five minutes to take the baby to the nursery. She needs a bottle. New mothers can take time to lactate," the nurse said gently. And as she said, she was back in five minutes. Helen gently kissed the baby as she handed the baby over to the nurse.

Helen woke up around 7 a.m. when the nurse came to check on her and brought the baby back for feeding. Both her mother and father were there to visit. Her mother cried as she held the baby. Helen's father looked choked up. He didn't say anything and didn't hold the baby. Peter came in at 7:30 a.m. It was the first time Helen's parents met him. Helen's father nodded as he said hello.

"Oh God, Helen, he is really old." Helen's mother knew that Peter was older than Helen but couldn't contain her surprise or disappointment. And she cried more.

Peter didn't look at the baby at first. "Are you ok?" he asked Helen. Helen nodded. She desperately wanted to talk to Peter but didn't want to do so in front of her parents.

"Peter, do you want to hold her?" Helen asked, and Peter looked startled. Just then the nurse came back to take the baby for a test. Helen saw Peter glance at the baby as her mother handed her over to the nurse. Peter closed his eyes and took a sharp breath as if he was in pain.

"Peter, how is this whole thing going to work out now?" Helen's father went over to Peter and whispered. He didn't want Helen to hear him. He knew that it would be best for everyone if they didn't spend much time with the baby.

"The De Silvas will be here soon. I called them," Peter said as he walked away with Helen's father. There was a strain in Peter's voice and Helen's father recognized that.

"Are you having second thoughts?" he asked Peter directly.

"No." Peter shook his head. But he wasn't so sure

anymore. He didn't expect himself to feel any different once the baby was born. But seeing her, it changed everything. He wasn't keen on seeing the baby, but he never stopped to think if he would feel any different. Peter was so focused on his plan to somehow make a life with Anoma, the fact that an actual baby might change how he felt had not even occurred to him. But when he saw the baby, cradled in Helen's mother's arms, he was shaken. He felt an instant pull. He wanted to look at her again but was afraid. It was not just a baby that had no image anymore. She was there, in flesh and blood, his flesh and blood. Peter was shaking. He didn't know what he wanted anymore.

"Peter." Just then, someone called out his name. Anura and Sriya were walking towards him. They had rushed to the hospital as soon as they got his call, their faces flushed with excitement and anticipation.

"Can we see the baby?" Peter nodded, trying to pull himself together. They walked together to the nursery and the nurse pointed out the baby to them. There were quite a few babies in the nursery.

Peter stood back, looking at the little baby girl. He felt a lump in his throat, and tears filled his eyes. "What am I doing, oh God, what the hell am I doing?" Peter saw Anura and Sriya holding each other with so much happiness, looking at this little baby girl. There was so much love already. Peter felt sick to his stomach.

"Where's Peter?" Helen asked as her father walked in. He looked drained and Helen sensed something was off.

"Peter is with that couple." Helen's father didn't name Anura and Sriya. But Helen understood. She felt as if the weight of the whole world just crashed on her chest. She couldn't breathe. She was screaming in her head, "No, please, no, I can't give her up. They can't take her," but she couldn't get the words out. She was sobbing so hard all she could say was "No…please, no."

Helen's mother put her arms around her grieving child. She saw the little girl she held so close to her heart and raised breaking down into pieces. She wished she could take her pain; she wished that Helen's husband would change his mind. But all she could do was hold her daughter and cry with her.

When Peter walked in with the adoption papers in hand, Helen's father walked out. He couldn't see his daughter in so much pain like this. He knew he was a tough father. He didn't always show his love with hugs and kisses or even words. But he loved his kids. He would do anything for them. He could never imagine giving up any of his children. But Peter was Helen's husband, and she must listen to him. This was their decision, their choice. Everyone must bear the consequences of their actions. That is the law of the world he came from.

"Please, Peter, please. You saw the baby. It's our baby. Please don't make me do this," Helen begged. But Peter simply shook his head.

"Mom, I can raise the baby. I have a job. I don't need money from anyone. Mom, please come with me. You can help me, please."Helen pleaded with her mother, grabbing her arm. Helen's mother didn't say anything but cried with her.

"You have to do what your husband says." Helen didn't see her father come back. Other people in the ward around them were looking at them now. They were whispering. But Helen could care less. She looked at Peter as he came closer and put the papers down. Helen looked at him pleadingly and saw that he had tears in his eyes as well. But he hasn't changed his mind. He had already signed the papers. Whatever he felt, regret, love , pain whatever it is, it wasn't enough to change his mind. Helen's mother got up and walked away, sensing that Peter and Helen needed to talk.

"Can you not change your heart, Peter?" Helen asked through tears.

"It is for the best Helen. This baby deserves better than us, better than me." His voice was hoarse. Helen looked at Peter. He looked tired and old. She saw other couples, new mothers and fathers smiling, holding their babies dotingly. There was love, so much around them. New fathers in awe of their wives, their hearts filled with love for the women who gave them the greatest gift in the world, a child. Yet all that love or happiness wasn't enough to break the wall this man had built. Or was it that his love for Anoma was bigger than his love for his own child?

Helen felt anger bubbling in her heart. She realized then that no matter what she did, Peter would never love her like he loved Anoma. No matter how hard she tries she will never be able to give a happy home to her child. There will always be a void. Her bed was the only one that didn't have a baby in it. It dawned on her that Peter had already notified the hospital of the adoption. Nurses hadn't brought her baby back from the nursery. She looked at Peter standing beside her and wondered how she could have been so wrong. This man was cruel, selfish. A monster who tore a child away from her mother. Her child was better off without him. Helen knew that Anuara and Sriya could give her baby what she could not, a happy stable family, two parents who love her.

Helen wiped her tears and grabbed the pen from Peter and signed the papers. "Here, you're right. My baby deserves much better than you." Helen thrusted the signed papers into Peter's hand. "Now you can go back to your mother and your family and continue to be the self-righteous asshole you are…but know this, I will never agree to a divorce. I gave up my child so that you can save your reputation. You can live your lie. But that life will be with me as my husband."

CHAPTER 22
Last Song

Peter didn't go back to the ward after handing the signed adoption papers to the De Silvas. He felt slightly dazed as he shook hands with Anura, who looked positively elated.

"You and Helen can come visit the baby. Thank you, Peter, thank you," Anura said repeatedly. He couldn't say anything. Peter searched for words, but his brain was in a fog, frozen in a state of turmoil, and he couldn't really put any of it into words. He just wanted to get away from there. He turned and left as soon as Anura turned back to go to his wife and their daughter. But before turning the corner Peter turned back to take one last look towards the nursery. He couldn't see the baby, but he saw Anura and Sriya holding a bundle in their hands. They looked so happy. Sriya looked like she was crying. Peter knew those were happy tears.

Then he left.

During the taxi ride back to his room, Peter stared out the window looking at passing lights, people walking about, stray dogs here and there. The streets were busy and bustling with life. But Peter felt empty. He felt like he had lived a thousand years and carried the weight of a thousand lives.

"Sir, sir. We are here." He heard the taxi driver and realized that they had arrived at the college residence.

"Thank you," he muttered as he paid the driver and turned back to walk into his room. The first thing he saw was Anoma's picture in a frame on his desk. He slowly walked to the table, picked up the frame and removed the picture. Peter ran his index finger across Anoma's face as he walked back to his bed and sank in. This woman, the love of his life, he had fought so hard for. Loved her his whole life. Lost her, found her again, and all he wanted was to spend the rest of his life with her. But now after everything, here he was looking at her picture and all Peter could think of was Helen's tearful face. How she begged and pleaded with her mother: "Just come with me, Mom, I could raise her on my own." He felt disgusted.

After all this, hurting everyone, he was here at this crossroad, and he knew what his choice should be. He knew then that even if he got the divorce, he couldn't leave what he did in the past. Suddenly Anoma felt like a mere memory. He knew that as much as he loved Anoma, any chance of them having a life together died that day with the adoption papers. The weight of what he had done, what he had forced Helen to do, would forever haunt him. He couldn't wash his sins away. He took a child from her mother. Helen will forever be scarred, and he owed it to her to share that grief. There was no other way. Peter knew without a doubt at that moment, his dreams, his wishes, the life he willed, were lost. His dreams were never a part of his destiny. He crumpled Anoma's picture in his hand as tears trickled down his face. He wasn't sure if he was grieving his lost dreams, the life he was destined for or a child he fathered but will never be a father to. Afterall, was he that different from his own father? He gave in to the blinding sorrow that took over him and sobbed.

He threw Anoma's picture across the room, which fell near his English mandolin. Peter slowly got up, picked up the mandolin and sat down by the window. This battered instrument had been his companion through many ups and downs. He had drowned his sorrows in its strings. Peter started humming softly, a hymn that felt sad yet strangely comforting as if it understood him:

Rock of Ages, cleft for me,

Let me hide myself in Thee;

Let the water and the blood,

From Thy riven side which flowed,

Be of sin the double cure,

Save me from its guilt and power..

He sang but his fingers couldn't strum the tune on his beloved mandolin. Peter's fingers felt numb. This lifeless instrument which has been a part of his life felt cold and strange. Frustrated, Peter got up and flung the mandolin out the window. He heard a thud and an odd sound as the mandolin splintered into pieces. And that was the end of a life, his life as he once knew. Peter got up, went to his desk, and pulled a notepad.

Peter didn't have to think anything over. Through the enormous grief he felt, his old self, the man he once was, found his way back. There was a sense of peace in that. He knew what he needed to do. As he started writing a letter to Anoma, Peter realized for the first time in months that he didn't have to lie. Through the sadness of it all he felt relieved, relieved that finally he could be honest. Honest with himself, Anoma and even Helen. Anoma and he were never meant to be. He realized that now. It was a dream, a dream he wanted so badly to be fulfilled but was not meant to be. His future was with Helen, a woman he had fought so hard to get away from. But at the end, Helen was the woman he was destined to be with. Not the woman he loved or chose but the woman fate has chosen.

They were brought together by fate. A fate he had fought so hard, stupidly believing that he could write his own story. How naïve was he? At the end they had all lost. Anoma, Peter, Helen, the baby, they were all simply pawns of a game of chess in which the winner had already been decided. It was always decided. A game between dreams and destiny played simply for the amusement of the gods, rigged in favor of destiny.

Peter put the letter in an airmail envelope, sealed it and wrote Anoma's address.

"I love you, Anom. You were the woman I wanted to spend the rest of my life with. What happened with Helen was a mistake. I never wanted to or planned to cheat on you. You asked me if it was revenge for you leaving me once. It wasn't. I hope you believe that. Had Helen not gotten pregnant, we may still have had a chance. But that was not our destiny. God had other plans. I tried fighting it and it cost us all so much. Forgive me for the pain I caused you. I made Helen give up her child, our child. It is not something I can walk away from. I must carry that burden and help her through that. I owe it to her.

I know I have no right to ask you for anything, but I beg you to protect this secret. I cannot undo this, and if my family finds out this secret it will only add to the burden I forced Helen to carry. I beg of you, please do not tell anyone about the baby. This baby is pure and innocent. She has a chance of living a good life untouched by all my sins. So please, please protect her secret. Do this not for me but for those who are innocent victims of my foolishness.

I hope you will find the happiness and love you deserve!

God bless,
Peter

Peter's heart was heavy yet clear. His future was with Helen. He was under no illusion that it was going to be all roses and sunshine. There was so much hurt, and both were deeply scarred. But their lives were intertwined together. Through their shattered dreams they would have to learn to piece together a new dream. They may even learn to love each other. "Love," what a strange thing, thought Peter sadly. He had felt so much happiness, an immeasurable amount of pain, frustration, anger, all sorts of intense feelings because of love. But after all that, love just felt like an insignificant word which stirred nothing in him. Just an empty word. Helen had told him she loved him.

At the time he was convinced that it was more of an infatuation which would soon come to pass. Even if it wasn't just an infatuation, after everything he had put her through, how could she feel anything other than hatred towards him? After all, there was only a thin line between love and hate.

Peter got up early the next day. He must have fallen asleep around 3 a.m. He was tired but his mind was sharp. Helen would be discharged today, and he needed to get to the hospital. Helen was going to stay with Padma for a few days. They hadn't discussed what was going to happen after. He had been so preoccupied with the adoption and his plans of convincing Helen to give him a divorce afterwards that he hadn't stopped to think that Helen might not agree to a divorce. He really didn't think of planning a life together with Helen.

When he got to the hospital Helen's mother and sister were already there. They had brought her breakfast, but the full plate told him that Helen hadn't even touched it. Helen greeted him as he came in, but he could feel her resentment. She wasn't crying anymore but her eyes looked sad and lost. Helen's mother and the sister were both polite towards him. They didn't stay long after he arrived. Peter was glad that they didn't as it gave him time to talk to Helen. They needed to figure out a lot of things.

"Helen, I spoke to Mel. We can stay with him until you are ready."

Helen looked at Peter with a puzzled look. "Ready for what?" she frowned. Helen felt her heart palpitating. Peter sensed the fear in her voice and gently took her hands between his.

"Ready to go home with me." Helen was taken aback. She looked at Peter. Did she hear him right? Helen searched for words but couldn't find any. She had fought for this, so hard for so long. To be his wife, to make a home with him. Finally, he was ready to be her husband, telling her she got her wish, but she didn't have anything to say to him. She didn't feel giddy with happiness, or her heart didn't leap with joy. Amidst the sadness of losing her child she hadn't thought what would happen next. She felt relieved that at last she wouldn't be abandoned, but that was all she felt: relief.

"When?" Helen asked as she pulled herself up.

"I was thinking about the end of July or August? Mel said it might be best to give you a month or two to recover," Peter continued cautiously.

Considering that my mother...my family doesn't know about..." He couldn't say the word baby. He sensed the tension in the air, raw and palpable. He stood up and walked around to the end of the bed and looked at Helen directly, holding the bed frame tightly, almost as if he needed the support.

"Helen, so much has happened; we can't change that. My family doesn't need to know any of this. I will take you home, as my wife. I…we will tell my mother that we got married without telling anyone because of my situation, you know, being a lecturer and all that. She won't question us. It is better this way. We can have a fresh start."

Helen nodded. A fresh start. What will it be like? Helen tried to think about it later after Peter left but she couldn't. She couldn't imagine the two of them as a couple, walking along the beach, holding hands doing things that couples do. Even when she forced herself to think of the two of them it felt unreal. So much had happened. Peter was right about that. She hated him for forcing her to give up the baby. She was angry at her mother for not agreeing to help her raise the baby. She hated Anoma for being loved by Peter, and she resented his family for forcing them to live a lie. She didn't care if her anger towards any of them was justified. That's all she seemed to be capable of feeling, anger. She was angry at the whole world.

On August 26, 1973, Helen stood in Melvin's living room. She was donned in a light blue georgette saree with white flowers. She was bidding goodbye to Melvin, his wife and their two children.

"Thanks for everything." Peter hugged Melvin as he took the two suitcases Helen had packed. Peter was finally taking Helen home to meet his mother.

Peter had gone home a week after Helen was discharged from the hospital and moved in with Melvin and his wife temporarily. He told his mother first and then the rest of his family about Helen. He told them that he fell in love with Helen and that was the reason Anoma and he broke up. His family was surprised, but they weren't all that sorry he broke up with Anoma. It turned out that none of them, especially his mother, never truly forgave Anoma for breaking his heart the first time. They only accepted her because they thought that's what Peter wanted. Alice was happy that her precious son was not settling for a divorcee. They weren't thrilled to hear that Peter and Helen were already married and denied them a wedding but soon got over it.

"Ready?" Peter asked Helen as he started the car. Helen smiled and nodded. Here they were: at their new beginning. Not how either one of them imagined it. There were no wedding bells, flowers or guests showering them with blessings. Instead, both looked on silently, lost in their own thoughts.

Helen was apprehensive of the fact that she was going into a whole new world. In the past few weeks Peter had opened up to her about his family, sharing a few stories from his childhood. Helen realized how little she knew about him and this world of his. She was acutely aware of the fact that the life they were building was based on secrets and lies. She didn't know much about Peter's mother, but it was clear that he adored her. She sensed that their secret, their child they gave up, was not something that will ever be forgiven should it come to light. Her own guilt and the fear of being exposed weighed heavily on her. Her dreams of romance, a grand wedding, a future with a man who will fulfill her desires felt like nothing more than a fairy tale she once read.

Peter had accepted his future with Helen as the gods will the day he signed the adoption papers. Every now and then, Anoma and the love he lost snuck into his mind, bringing a tear to his eyes. But he didn't ponder those thoughts. He had accepted what was written in his cards. He had fought for his dreams and lost. The cost of that fight weighed heavily on him. He knew that he would carry it to the end of his days. Peter thought he was prepared for this day. But as the car rolled through the busy streets, he felt fearful. "God always has a plan. Trust in him. There's no point of worrying too much." His brother's words rang in his mind. That was his brother's answer to all his problems. It used to annoy Peter. His brother with seven kids and a wife depending solely on his pension always took solace in trusting in God's plan while Peter worried and fretted about his nephews and nieces. Perhaps he was right, thought Peter with a sigh.

"We are here," Peter said as they pulled in front of an old house with whitewashed pillars and a tiled roof. There was a tall, dark, lean woman with gray hair on the veranda. She got up as the car pulled to a stop.

"That's my mother," said Peter. Helen looked and saw the woman walking towards them with a big smile looking exuberant. She looked old and worn out, the hardships of the life she lived visible on her face. Yet there was a warmth about this woman that said it was all worth it.

As Helen got out of the car she wondered if she would ever feel that kind of happiness. Peter's mother hugged Helen and then moved to hug Peter. She then forcibly took one bag from her son and walked back to the house. "Don't just stand there, Peter, bring your wife into the house."

Helen felt relieved as she stood watching this older woman who seemed simply happy for her son and his new bride. Helen took a deep breath, smelling the fragrant white flowers of coffee plants along the hedge. It reminded her of Sepalika flowers at home.

Peter held a hand out to her, ready to walk into a world that was forced upon them. Helen and Peter stood there, hand in hand, finally embracing their destiny. A future that was designed for them from pieces of their broken dreams held together by feeble threads of survival and guilt. Together they walked with shadows of their past trailing behind, never really leaving them.

CHAPTER 23
Blood Is Thicker Than Water

Mala pulled into the underground car park at One-Galle Face Mall. She was anxious. She told her husband that she was going to meet her school friends. A reunion with a friend visiting from abroad. It wasn't a lie altogether; she was going to meet her friend Mano tomorrow along with some of her classmates. But today she was here for a different reason.

Today she was here to meet Sakura and Nevan, her biological brother and sister.

It had been four months since she received an email from Sakura telling her that she was her sister. Mala was devastated. She hadn't wanted to believe it. Sakura had offered to take a DNA test to prove they were sisters. But Mala didn't need that. She knew as she read the email that it was true. She had never had a reason to doubt her existence, her parents. But all the same, she just knew what was written in that email was true. Her parents were both dead so she couldn't ask them. It made sense to take a DNA test, just to be sure. Yet in her heart she knew it was true. It all made sense. She looked at the picture of Sakura's parents on her Facebook. Her biological parents: Aunty Helen and Uncle Peter as she remembered them. Mala saw the resemblances.

Mala had cried the whole night she found out. She had almost told her husband, but she didn't. She didn't know how he would handle this piece of information. Mala's world as she knew it had turned upside down. She felt like a stranger, and she didn't know how her husband would take it. She was afraid of rejection. She knew that he was very much a byproduct of a judgmental society rather unforgiving of those who stray from the social norms.

His mother had always been respectful of her and accepted her readily into their folds. But Mala had had no illusions to the fact that it would have been a very different story had it not been for her sizable dowry and for being the sole heiress to her parents' wealth. But it had surprised her when she realized that her husband was no different. Of course, he didn't love her for her wealth, and it probably would have made no difference to him, at least when they were younger, but now that their sons were young adults she was surprised to hear her husband talk about them finding a "suitable wife." It had irked her when he had vehemently opposed their older son's choice of a girl who came from a family that used to work in his grandparents' coconut estate. The fact that this girl was educated and made her son happy made no difference to her husband. Mala had argued with him. She was disappointed, more so in herself for not knowing him. In the end it didn't matter. Kids were young and they had drifted apart.

She also remembered how her husband reacted to his sister when she fell in love with a young man about ten years ago. Her sister-in-law was a widow. She had gotten married young, against the will of her parents, to a soldier. He had died in the war. They had no children. Mala had never seen her sister-in-law, Anula, that happy. Anu met this young man, Hiran, who had just moved to town working as a branch manager at a bank. Hiran was the middle son of a family of three boys. His parents had flipped as soon as they found out that Anu was a widow. They had called her "secondhand goods." The sad part was that her husband and his family didn't fight for their daughter. "Anu, you should look for someone suitable for your situation" was the response of her mother-in-law. Her situation being a widow. And suitable men were those who were divorced, widowed themselves or old. When Mala tried to explain that calling her secondhand goods was not something you should accept, her husband's response was "What would you do if it was our sons?"

She understood her husband and his family. And she herself had biases, she knew that. Mala was afraid that the moment her husband found out that she was adopted, it would change the way he looked at her. She knew that her mother-in-law would consider this a betrayal, never mind the fact that it was really Mala who was betrayed. Even her husband, she suspected, wouldn't take it kindly.

Overall, he had been a good husband to her. He had financially supported her, been a good father to their sons and a good son in law to her parents. He was there when she lost her parents. And she wouldn't have been able to get through it all without him. But the truth was that was all they were to each other. A support system. Even at the beginning of their marriage, it was more of a comfort with little passion. Overtime, the passion died, and they fell into their respective roles: husband and wife. Two people who promised to stay together. It had worked for them. They had simple and straightforward lives. Until now.

Mala had agonized over this secret since she found out. She felt like she was cheating on her husband. But every time she thought of confiding in her husband, she had played all the possible outcomes. And none of them had been positive. In the end, she had decided to tell no one, not even her best friend. Finally, she decided to meet her sister by herself. So, she replied to the email. It had taken several days and about hundred deleted drafts before she finally managed to compile one. It was short:

Hello Sakura,

Sorry it took this long to respond. I'm sure you can imagine how shocked I was at first. But truth be told it sort of made sense in a weird way. I'm still processing this, and I appreciate you keeping this to yourself. I have a lot of questions, perhaps we can chat?

Best,
Mala

Sakura had responded immediately and had sent a Facebook friend request. After that they started chatting, and Mala found it got easier. Ruwan had asked a few times who she was chatting with, and she just said it was a friend in Canada. He left it at that.

Finally, Sakura had asked if Mala would be open to meeting her and her brother in person. Mala had said yes, but she had said that it would be just her. She wasn't ready to tell her husband or her sons yet. She didn't tell Sakura that she was afraid of her husband's reaction. Mala wasn't ready to share that kind of information about her life or her loved ones with Sakura or Nevan yet. After all this is still new territory for her and for them.

It was December and One Galle Face was buzzing with Christmas shoppers. Mala was meeting Sakura and Nevan at the Shangri-la. They had planned to meet for high tea. Her sister and brother had flown in a few days ago to meet her. She was anxious and wanted to calm her nerves. So she decided to come early and just walk around the mall before heading to the hotel lobby. Finally she made her way into Sapphyr Lounge. She was nervous and wished she wasn't alone. As she walked in, she immediately saw Sakura and Nevan. She recognized them from their Facebook pictures.

Mala felt awkward at first and wished her husband was there with her. Sakura came with open arms and embraced Mala as if they had known each other their whole life, and Nevan joined in. Soon they were hugging each other. They stood there embracing each other, trying to bridge more than half a century of their lives, experiences and moments lost. Then Sakura and Nevan walked Mala towards their table where the rest of their families stood. Sakura's husband and daughter and Nevan's wife and the two kids, a son and daughter, all looking eagerly at her, beaming with welcoming smiles. And at that moment, Mala knew that all would be fine. She knew that she was not alone, that she had a brother and a sister. She knew what she was going to do. She would tell her family. She knew that her boys would never think less of her. She had raised them better than that. And it didn't matter if her husband wouldn't accept who she is. She was not alone.

Finally, after 53 years, Mala felt complete. Her life as she knew it was no more, but the life ahead was full of possibilities and dreams that promised a happy ending.

AUTHOR'S NOTE

Dear reader,

Thank you for going on this journey of Helen, Peter, Mala, Sakura and Nevan with me. Well, now you have reached the end of the book, you've taken the road that Helen and Peter walked.

I hope you felt the heartbeat of Helen, the pain of being forced to give up her child, having to contend with watching her first born from a distance as a mere spectator. I hope you understood her grief, her broken heart, loss of innocence and the bitterness of the unfulfilled life she chose to live.

I also hope you understood Peter, a man who surely sinned. Who did something unthinkable. He strayed and betrayed a sacred trust, and he took a child from her mother. He acted selfishly. But is that all he was? Does that take away from the undoubtedly great father he was to Sakura and Nevan? Does it take away from the great and respected teacher that he was to many? Does it diminish what a great uncle, brother, and son he was? Does it take away the remarkable man he otherwise was throughout his life? Does it diminish the pain of having to watch his first born also as a mere spectator from the sidelines? These questions live in the reality that he knowingly made these decisions.

When I started writing this story, my intention was to give my readers a novel, a story, fiction loosely based on true events. But as I dove into it, I realized it was more than just a fictional novel. It was a story of many women, mothers across the world who were forced to give up their babies. A decision forced on them and not a choice. I found myself immersed in the characters, wondering how it feels not to have the freedom to choose? How would it feel to be a victim of a judgemental society?

I look at women around me today who enjoy the freedom of choice, independence and societal support and, should they find themselves in Helen's predicament, raising a child on their own, would have a viable, judgment-free option. It would not condemn them or their children to being treated any less. Then I look into other parts of the society, both near and far, and see people across the world who become the judge and jury. Condemning both the woman and the child. I think of Mala, who stands to lose her status in the society due to no fault of her own but simply for being an adopted child.

Writing this story made me think of all the men and women I know who had fallen prey to societal judgments: smart beautiful, accomplished women, a woman earning a high six figure salary, going head to head in the male-dominated corporate world and winning, yet silently suffering in a mentally and physically abusive marriage due to valuing social acceptance more than her self worth.

A woman who is intelligent and progressive, who rose above childhood abuse yet silently bowed her head when the very person she trusted called her "secondhand goods." A man who took his own life because he lived in a society where he couldn't love another man and be true to himself since he neither had the money or the power to rise above societal judgements. My heart aches for all those who feel the need to hide their past, rip up pictures of their college lives for they bore evidence of them having fun, having a drink, experiencing romance, and living their lives, for it is not acceptable to the life awaiting them back home where they must conform to being a future good wife and a daughter-in-law.

We are all guilty of being a part of that judgemental society. I know I am. We all are governed by the norms and expectations of the society we live in, by our beliefs and or our upbringings. I hope this book makes you stop and think next time you find yourself ready to judge another. Cultural values should not be a barrier to progress. If the values you hold victimize others, then they are not values. A culture that hinders societal evolution has already failed. Educating children on their reproductive rights, giving them the tools and knowledge to protect them when making the right choice, is not robbing them of their innocence. Empowering women is not emasculating men.

In the end, writing this book was a journey for me. It was cathartic. My hope is that this story provides you enjoyment while at the same time being a voice to all the Helens and Malas in the world.

Xo Xo : Nadee

MEET NADEE FERNANDO-O'DRISCOLL

A mother, a wife, a daughter, a sister, a friend and a colleague and now an author. She is a woman who writes her own story, dances to her own tune and sings her own song (off-key I must add).

Nadee was born and raised in Sri Lanka and obtained her Bachelor of Science from the University of Pune, India. She moved to Ottawa, Canada in 2004 and now lives in beautiful Carleton Place with her daughter, husband, two cats and dog. Nadee and her husband have two other adult children who are writing their own success stories in the world. Nadee loves sharing her life and passions with her husband, children and their precious granddaughter.

Although she always had a knack for writing, it wasn't until she was 49 that she thought about writing a novel. She always felt strongly about social pressures and conventions- particularly in socially conservative countries being somewhat of an unconventional woman herself. Writing this novel, her debut, made her realize that she had a passion for writing. It filled a void she felt in her life. Mostly this particular novel gave her a platform to highlight the struggles of people, women in particular, due to archaic social biases.

Embracing this new chapter in her life, she is determined to be an example of defying dogmatism within conventional societies, to show that it is never too late to dream a new dream, that one doesn't have to be defined by failures but rather by how one overcomes them.

- Email: nadee.g.f@gmail.com
- Website: https://nadeefernando-odriscoll.com/
- Instagram: https://www.instagram.com/f.nadee
- LinkedIn: https://www.linkedin.com/in/nadee-fernando-089a3a97/

thank you

THANK YOU
FOR READING MY BOOK

I really appreciate all of your feedback and I love hearing what you have to say.

I need your input to make the next version of this book and my future books better. Please take two minutes now and leave a helpful review on Amazon letting me know what you thought of the book.

Thanks so much!

Nadee

MY GIFT TO YOU

I am so glad you're here!

As my Gift to you, get FREE Access to the
Audiobook Labyrinth of Dreams
by scanning the QR Code below or visiting

https://nadeefernando-odriscoll.com/